SWAY of the SIREN

a novel

L.K. McCall

a may river press llc. publication

Email: swayofthesiren@gmail.com Website: www.swayofthesiren.com

Cover art and design by Eric McCall.

Author photo by Ann K. Cothran.

Grateful acknowledgment is made to Josh Garrels for permission to reprint previously published material:

Lyrics from the song "Anchor" from the album *Love & War: B-Sides & Remixes* by Josh Garrels copyright © 2012 by Josh Garrels. Reprinted by permission of Josh Garrels.

Lyrics from the song "Beyond the Blue" from the album *Love & War & The Sea In Between* by Josh Garrels copyright © 2011 by Josh Garrels. Reprinted by permission of Josh Garrels.

Lyrics from the song "Bread and Wine" from the album *Love & War & The Sea In Between* by Josh Garrels copyright © 2011 by Josh Garrels. Reprinted by permission of Josh Garrels.

Lyrics from the song "Farther Along" from the album *Love & War & The Sea In Between* by Josh Garrels copyright © 2011 by Josh Garrels. Reprinted by permission of Josh Garrels.

Lyrics from the song "Flood Waters" from the album *Love & War & The Sea In Between* by Josh Garrels copyright © 2011 by Josh Garrels. Reprinted by permission of Josh Garrels.

Lyrics from the song "Just Doin' Your Thing" from the album *Lost Animals* by Josh Garrels copyright © 2009 by Josh Garrels. Reprinted by permission of Josh Garrels.

Lyrics from the song "Million Miles" from the album *Love & War & The Sea In Between* by Josh Garrels copyright © 2011 by Josh Garrels. Reprinted by permission of Josh Garrels.

Lyrics from the song "Slip Away" from the album *Love & War & The Sea In Between* by Josh Garrels copyright © 2011 by Josh Garrels. Reprinted by permission of Josh Garrels.

Lyrics from the song "The Resistance" from the album *Love & War & The Sea In Between* by Josh Garrels copyright © 2011 by Josh Garrels. Reprinted by permission of Josh Garrels.

Lyrics from the song "Ulysses" from the album *Love & War & The Sea In Between* by Josh Garrels copyright © 2011 by Josh Garrels. Reprinted by permission of Josh Garrels.

ISBN 978-0-9968217-0-4

To my true love
who carried me back home
again and again.

God wastes nothing.

Acknowledgements

I'm thankful for my savior, Jesus Christ, whose unfathomable love has never let me go.

Thank you, Eric McCall for living out the gospel, so that I could know God's love on this side of heaven. I love you. "I've been changed by what I've been shown, more glory than the world has ever known." – Josh Garrels

Gabe and Joey, I love you. Thank you for giving me time and space to create. Always remember that on your worst day, God's love for you is deeper than the ocean and wider than the universe. You are known and loved.

With special thanks to Elijah Heyward, Jr., my mentor, muse and friend whose criticism helped me as much as his encouragement. Thank you for sharing stories of your culture and giving me glimpses into such a rich heritage. I could not have written this book without you.

Thank you to my parents, Roger and Mary Ellen Kellogg, for their encouragement, love, and support.

John Ring, thank you for your compassion and for reminding me of the gospel over and over and over again.

Thank you to each of the members of my writers' group, Laura Wilson, Regina Mae, Melinda Copp, and Stephanie Bente, for being the coolest group of women on the planet.

Joanie Coleman, you are absolutely resolutely the best beta reader the world has ever known. Thank you for your countless hours of feedback and mad editing skills.

Lalie Mole, thank you for showing me unconditional love and support. Thank you for sharing your stories with me. Most of all, thank you for showing me through example what it means to walk by faith.

Katie Holcombe, thanks for being a faithful friend, for sharing your heart, for walking me home, for being beautiful you.

SWAY of the SIREN

My story begins with the Gullah/ Geechee version of Adam and Eve. I first heard this particular version as it was recited by Lenora Eve. Lenora learned the story from her father, Paul Eve who used to tell it to her at many a bedtime. Paul grew up on the Eve Farm, now Habersham, in Beaufort, SC. Her father, Paul, learned the story from a local friend that he played with growing up. I would like to thank Lenora for helping me to transcribe the story. The original credit belongs to the Gullah/ Geechee people who have such a beautiful heritage of oral tradition. The Gullah/ Geechee people are the most gifted storytellers I've ever heard. They use such tales to entertain and to teach.

Where did I go wrong? I sang along to every chorus of the song that the devil wrote like a piper at the gates, leading mice and men down to their fates, but some courageously escape the seductive voice with a heart of faith while walkin' that line back home.

- Josh Garrels

1

Mabel eyed her grandson. "I ever tell you the story of Adam and Eve?"

"*Everybody* knows the story of Adam and Eve, Grandma," he said.

"No, Son. I mean the *real* story. Come with me." De'Andre and his younger brother Tyrone had lived with their grandmother since they were just arm babies, before the milk had dried from their mouths. De'Andre followed her out into the garden. He wandered down a well worn path between lush green rows of ripe squash and zucchini, towards the tomatoes bursting with color. He could smell the strawberries, his favorite, but he knew he better keep on moving. "Now, make yourself useful en pull dem weeds." He knew he was in trouble when she started telling stories in Gullah. The mosquitoes were already on him, but he didn't dare complain.

Mabel began weeding the garden alongside her

grandson. "Een de beginnin Gawd been make man en put em down dis gaden called de Gaden a Eden. Now e put em down der, tell em fuh enjoy all dem convenience round de gaden, fuh have a fine time. Now Adam been down der about two or tree day, finally been full a de pure lonesome. E ain't know wha fuh do, en de Lawd bust outta Hebben say, 'Adam, what ail ya?'"

"En e say, 'Ya know, Lawd, I been fix fuh ask ya de same ting.' En e say, 'What ail me, Lawd?'"

"En e say, 'Ya know, I tink ya need a ooman fuh look af'ya round dis gaden.' So e take a rib, en e hair, en make a ooman, en e name dat ooman Eve. En e say, 'Dere ain't one ting I ain't want ya fuh do. I ain't want ya fuh touch dem apple on dat tree, en I done count em en I know how many der.'"

"So Adam en Eve been makin friends wid all dem vamints round de gaden. Finally dey been talk fuh dat serpent, en dat serpent been coax em, en coax em, en coax em, want Eve fuh tas'suh apple. E say, 'Ya know dem apple *sho* must be good if de Lawd ain't want ya fuh tas'sum.'"

"So one day Adam sneak out en take one small bite off de apple. Soon e do, de lightenin been flash en de tunder been roll, en de Lawd bust outta Hebben en e called, 'Adam!'"

"En Adam been in dat fig tree, en dat fig tree been shakin, shakin, en shakin like a hurricane been hit em, en e say, 'Great day, I gotta get out dis gaden now.' So e take e foot in e hand, en e stretch out round dat gaden."

"Finally e peep o'er e shoulder en seen de Lawd been gainin on em. E make one more trip round dat gaden, en e see a hole een de fence where a hog been root, en e say, 'Next time I come roun here, I gonna try fuh get tru dat hole.' So e make one more trip roun dat gaden, make a dive fuh dat hole en e get stick, en de Lawd come behind him wid e gold axe. Ya know all God's tools been gold, ya know? Come up behind em wid e gold axe en chop off e tail. Dats why man ain't got no tail now fuh brush off fly en skeeter when e in de field fuh plow, or when e in de gaden fuh weed."

Mabel watched her grandson weed the garden while the story set in. She watched, hiding her smile as he smacked mosquitoes from the back of his neck and swung blindly at the no-see-ums. When the time was right she said, "Don't let me catch you near that creek by yourself no more. Gafa coulda got more than your tail comin' back across that river at high tide. You understand me?"

"Yes, Ma'am."

"Now there's more to that story, but the rest of it's a secret."

"Oh, I can keep a secret," De'Andre said.

"You sure 'bout that?"

"Yes, Ma'am," he declared with all the convincing in the world.

"Well, after Adam and Eve sinned, God cast everyone out of the garden forever, or that's what people think. You can't tell nobody, but Goethe is really Eden."

De'Andre stopped weeding, looking around at the beauty of the land that was sculpted by the hard working hands of his ancestors and the ditch that surrounded the island. His grandmother had told him the story of how his ancestors had dug that ditch, dug it down *deep* to surround Goethe like a mental moat, to remind each of them that survival over slavery and perseverance over ignorance should never be forgotten. He thought about what he knew about Eden. "No it's not," he laughed.

"Yeah it is. Think about it. It's where all the white folks been cast out by the sins of their ancestors."

"There's still white people here, Grandma."

Mabel ran several guest cottages in Honey Hill, the last remaining Gullah community on Goethe Island. The guests at The Cottages varied, but more and more the white folk came. Each one felt like a threat to the last bit of land that the ancestors had managed to hold on to. She tried to embrace the tourism, harnessing the income that came with it while protecting everything about the island, an impossible balance.

The income from The Cottages was about the only way to keep up with the property taxes which had increased by six hundred percent over the last year thanks to a few rich white folks who had come in and built million dollar houses right next to local trailers and run down homes, homes that had once stood as proud promises of a future of freedom and generations later bowed under the same old weight of oppression. White folks, whose investors told them how their money would grow exponentially as the island was transformed into a private country club, moved in like maggots eating away the decay, saving the place from ruin.

"A few of 'em found their way back, but that's why it's important that we hold on to our land. Hold on to it tight. Never let it go. You know that giant moss covered oak tree you swing on all the time?"

"Yes, Ma'am."

"Look up at her trunk next time, where her bark still bears the scarred stripes of the lashings, testifying to the trials and tribulations, been singing the same spirituals for over a century."

"That don't sound like heaven to me," De'Andre said.

"Your ancestors were strong, and that means you are strong. They were survivors, and that means you are a miracle, but there's more to it than that."

"Like what?"

"Goethe is where time slows down and technology drowns on the passage from the mainland, where the old folks hold on to the old ways of cast net fishin', community livin', everybody givin', where respect is earned and trust comes slowly, where the air is fresh and the roads aren't paved, where there is no crime and the kids can just play, where plankton glow like stars beneath your feet. Goethe is where our people are truly free."

"This is America, Grandma. Everybody's free."

"That's what you think. People become enslaved by all kinds of things, things they have and things they wanna have. Some people are ruled by their emotions—bitterness, fear, hate, even love. Freedom is something you have to protect." She smiled. "Now give me a hug and go wash up and get ready for bed."

The next morning it came to De'Andre clear as Gabriel's trumpet calling the saints to come home, raising him from the dead—the unmistakable, irresistible smell of bacon that drifted through the open window. There's nothing better. That is, unless you ain't allowed to eat it. He thought about the story his grandmother had told him the night before, but it was all about the creek and apples. She never said anything about bacon. De'Andre slid on his flip-flops and crept through the kitchen where leftover fish and grits from the night before were starting to pop and splatter across the stovetop like an active volcano. He could see his grandmother out in the garden picking fresh strawberries, and he knew he only had a few minutes to make a break for it before his little brother Tyrone would be on him like a tick, and he did not want to be stuck babysitting a kindergartner for half the day.

Sliding out the side door, he darted through the yard and around to the back of the nearest cottage to see what the guests had leftover from breakfast. He knew he'd get a whuppin' if his grandmother saw him, because in order to get some bacon, he'd have to break at least three rules:

1. You don't bother the guests.
2. You can speak to white folks, but you never hang around talking to them.
3. You don't ever eat white folks' cooking.

"Morning, Miss. My grandmother sent me by to see if you needed anything. Make sure you slept alright."

"You're so cute. John, look. Isn't he so cute? How old are you?"

"Seven and a half." He knew he'd have to endure a few questions. White people were always nosey, just like his grandmother had warned him.

"So you live here?" the lady asked.

"Yes, Ma'am."

"What's it like living on Goethe?"

"It's fun. I guess," he said.

"I think it would be like heaven living here. What can you tell me about Honey Hill?" the woman asked.

De'Andre knew lots about Honey Hill. He knew that it was the most special place on earth, where the land itself lived and breathed the stories and the lessons of his ancestors. Sometimes he would be outside playing, and he would hear his name whispered in the wind. He would stop moving and close his eyes, feeling the spirits warm on his face like the sun and at the same time cool on his skin like a breeze. He'd open his eyes to find his arms covered in goose bumps and know that he was not alone.

He knew that the elders feared losing the land, and if they ever did, it would change their way of life forever, change his life forever. He knew a lot. "What you wanna know?" he asked.

"You know if anybody's trying to sell their property?"

"Ain't nothing for sale 'round here, Ma'am."

"I've seen a few new houses. So I know places must occasionally come up for sale. I can only imagine what this land is worth. Think of the kind of house they could afford on the mainland if they just sold their property for what it's worth. Can you imagine that, John?" De'Andre shrugged his shoulders. "Well, you can tell your grandmother we slept very well. Hey, would you care for some breakfast? Bacon and chocolate chip pancakes," the lady offered in her most sing songy voice.

"Thank you, Ma'am. I wish I could. I *am* hungry, but my cousin's expectin' me at her place in a few minutes."

"Well, you still gotta eat, don't you? How 'bout some for the road?"

"Yes, Ma'am. That'd be awesome." De'Andre wondered how long this couple would stick around, because he could get used to this. It wasn't uncommon for white folks to plan to stay for a week and be gone after about two days. They'd show up at The Sandbar, the only bar on the island, and the whole atmosphere would change in an instant, only they would have no idea. The loud banter and laughing would cease, and locals would suddenly find themselves talking in quiet and sometimes unspoken code. White folks would be coming to see and experience the "culture," and what they didn't realize was that the most special thing about the culture was the very fact that there weren't any white people in it.

After about two days of very little interaction with anyone, plus no golf, no restaurants, no black folks on display weaving sweet grass baskets or doing The Ring Shout, and those folks would be on the next ferry back to the mainland, heading over to Hilton Head or Daufuskie. Those islands, where history could be divided into "before da' bridge" and "after da' bridge," were just a reminder to Mabel of all the things she was fighting so hard to save.

De'Andre left the cottage on his bike with a baggie full of chocolate chip pancakes and bacon and headed straight for his cousin Jasmine's. Even though she was a girl, and was a whole year younger, she was more daring than most boys his age, not to mention, she was one of the only kids on the island to play with except for his little brother.

De'Andre banged on Aunt Elanda's door. He knew that his Uncle Jedidiah, Uncle Jed for short, would already be at work at the docks.

"Is Jasmine up?"

"Lord, Child, whatcha doin' up so early? Ain't you want to sleep in the last few days a summer?"

"I don't know. I can't help it. I jus' wake up. She up yet?"

"She's eatin' breakfast and watchin' cartoons. Let me see if I can get her movin'."

Within minutes Jasmine was on her bike, and the two were peddling for the beach. Jasmine had a new bike she had just gotten for Christmas, and that thing was fast, maybe not as fast as De'Andre's bike, had he been tall enough to truly reach the pedals. He had not quite grown into the hand-me-down bike that had been around for so long he didn't even know where it had come from. He either had to balance on the seat, shifting his weight from right to left, waiting for the pedal to make its way around so he could give it a good solid push, or he could stay standing up on the pedals, but it was impossible to sit comfortably and pedal fast enough to keep up with Jasmine.

"Let's take the cut," Jasmine said, and without waiting for a response she was off, leading the way, as she did in most everything. "Race ya'," she yelled over her shoulder, the colorful beads in her hair bouncing off her back to the rhythm of the ruts in the road.

The cut was a well-cleared path through the woods, about a mile and a half with a mile walk down the beach to get to the pavilion, as opposed to three miles on the main road. De'Andre was following closely behind Jasmine, like trying to keep up with a wild horse, when all of a sudden she slammed on her brakes, bike skidding sideways on the dirt path, causing De'Andre to slam his chest into his handlebars just as his foot slipped off the pedal, which smacked him hard in the back of the leg. Jasmine stood silently staring off towards the sweet potato patch, the pride and joy of Goethe.

"Look, buzzards flyin' 'round! Somethin's dead!" she said.

Just then a slight breeze directed the distinct odor of death in their direction. There was no question. It reminded De'Andre of the time Blue's mule had died in the field, and all the men had been down on the north end of the island trying to put out a wildfire. They'd been working to keep the fire under control for four days straight, and it seemed like that dead mule stunk up half the island. By the time some of the men were freed up to bury that thing, the buzzards hadn't left anything but bones and the smell was gone.

"Let's go see! Come on, Dre!" She took off down a side path with De'Andre peddling as hard as he could, trying to keep up, legs burning.

"Hold up!" he yelled. The buzzards had yet to descend, boldly circling above them in the sky. The closer they got to the sweet potato patch, the stronger the smell became. De'Andre pulled his shirt collar up over his mouth and nose to try to filter the stench, and even then he fought hard against his gag reflex. Jasmine and De'Andre spotted the body at the same time. They looked at each other, and without a word each knew what the other was thinking. Jasmine wanted to get a closer look, and De'Andre wanted to go get help, not that there was much help to get. This was Goethe. The closest hospital was an airlift away to the mainland, not to mention this was clearly a dead body. There wasn't anything anyone could do to help.

Jasmine stopped, lowering her bike to the ground in slow motion, like she was afraid of waking the dead. Both stood perfectly still and silent for what seemed like several minutes out of reverence and fear of the first dead body either of them had ever seen. There, at the edge of the sweet potato patch, against a live oak, rested the body of what used to be a white woman. Now she was various shades of black, purple and gray. Her hand and forearm was black as Miss Annie's, but there was no doubt she was a white woman, or had been at one time. Her fingers had split open like hotdogs that had been held over the fire too long. Her grotesquely deformed arm rested oddly against her chest. The color faded from black to purple to gray as it moved away from her hand and up her body. Her eyes were closed, and she had a surprisingly peaceful expression on her face, like she might have been taking an afternoon nap when her arm decided to swell to the size and color of an overgrown eggplant in the middle of a sweet potato patch.

De'Andre looked up at the buzzards circling impatiently, waiting for their turn. A giant cloud of flies swarmed around the body like sentries, daring anyone to come close. Miss Rita had taught him the word "sentries" last school year, knowing he was smart enough for the fourth grade words. He liked the idea of the flies, or anything, any sign telling him not to go any closer, and he would've heeded the sentries' warning had it not been for Jasmine. Still, neither of them had moved an inch and neither had spoken up until that moment. Jasmine took one step forward, and then another, like he knew she would.

"Jazz, no! Don't touch her!"

"I ain't," Jasmine said, circling the dead body, not like the vultures above, but like a cat, stealthy and curious. De'Andre eyed Jasmine with as much wonder as he eyed the dead woman, how she could take it all in, immune to the smell and the sight. He took two steps, close enough to see that the skin on the dead body was moving like water in a pot just before it starts to boil. He thought his eyes were playing tricks on him, like the way a mirage causes the paved road to shimmer in the heat of day. As if Jasmine had read his mind, "It's maggots. She musta been dead for 'bout five, six hours now." Jasmine was on her own set of *CSI*. De'Andre began to gag, fell to his knees and threw up. He wished he hadn't stopped by the cottage.

"I think a bad man killed her," Jasmine said. This was Goethe. There weren't any "bad men" on Goethe. There were some drunks, lots of moonshine and a couple of hidden patches of marijuana growing on the island, but there wasn't any real crime on Goethe, certainly not murder. No one locked their doors or even took the keys out of their ignition, ever. De'Andre had been told stories about life on the mainland, but he also knew that Goethe was different.

More and more, people from the mainland were coming to the island. It was changing, parts of it being lost, and now there was a dead body. Maybe it had been a bad man, but definitely no descendants could've or would've done this.

"Jazz, we gotta go! We gotta tell somebody. Come on!"

"Wait, what you think happened?"

"I don't know, Jazz. We gotta go tell one of the elders."

"You think a bad man got her? That's what I think. What you think, Dre?"

"Jasmine, I don't know, but if it was a bad man he could still be here. We gotta go. *NOW*! Come on!"

"Dre, wait! There's something in her hand!"

For the first time, De'Andre was leading the way, only Jasmine wasn't following. He was off on his bike, peddling back towards The Cottages. Jasmine ventured closer, a dreadful curiosity drawing her to the body. It wasn't until she got within arm's reach that she recognized the woman, a Goethe Soul Sister, Maya. Slowly and carefully she reached for the hand, and then a feeling, a horrible feeling came over Jasmine, and she turned to find herself all alone with the dead body of a woman she had known and loved. Maya had been coming to the island for as long as Jasmine could remember. She became paralyzed with fear when a sudden movement and rustling of leaves revealed a toad that leaped up onto the dead woman's body, landing right on her incongruous arm. Jasmine screamed so loudly that De'Andre heard her halfway down the cut and was sure the bad man had gotten her too. Jasmine ran for her bike. She could still see De'Andre up ahead. He was stopped in the middle of the path, waiting for her. Jasmine was crying and shaking violently by the time she reached De'Andre.

"It's Maya, Miss Maya, my sista! She's my sista!" Jasmine let her bike drop to the ground, and De'Andre grabbed hold of her before she collapsed and held her as she sobbed and gasped for air, bearing her weight until she could breathe again.

"I don't know what happened, Jazz, but we gotta go get help. We gotta get outta here." Jasmine shook her head in agreement, sucking in short shallow breaths and wiping her nose on her arm. They both headed back up the cut together, peddling as fast as they could toward The Cottages to find Mabel.

Higher than the yonder mountain and deeper than the sea, from the breadth of the East unto the West is the love that started with a seed, stronger than the wildest horses and the rising tide. The chords of death hung so heavy on our necks will be left at the great divide. Flood waters rise, but it won't wash away. Love never dies. It will hold on more fierce than graves.

- Josh Garrels

2

Mabel

"What you mean there's a dead woman in the sweet potato patch?" Jasmine was talkin' a mile a minute, and De'Andre was jumpin' 'round behind her, 'bout to make me dizzy. She talked so fast I couldn't hardly understand her, and she had the craziest story I ever heard her tell 'bout a bad man and a purple woman with a swole up arm and a toad. De'Andre just shook his head with affirmation, but didn't say nothin'. "Get off that bed, Jazzy. What I tell you 'bout gettin' on the bed?"

"Grandma!"

I had just stripped the beds in the first cottage and had four more cottages to go before the next guests arrived on the five o'clock ferry. We had a couple comin' from Alabama to make a documentary 'bout Goethe and the property tax issues, and I had to make sure all the rooms was ready. We also had five chefs comin' from Hilton Head Island to have a Sweet Potato Cook-off at the Community Center, all part of the documentary. This was free publicity for *Yam Bam Spirits*, GIPS's (Goethe Island Preservation Society's) hope to raise money to help the descendants pay their property taxes for the upcoming year.

Goethe's first pride was Amelia Riley, Juilliard alumna and soloist with the American Ballet Theatre, but the sweet potato patch was a close second. Everybody will tell you, sweet potatoes grow best where the sand is salty and the rainwater is sacred and the real secret is simple as faith. The term "sweet potato" couldn't be any more bitter for some folks who insisted that it was a yam that sustained our ancestors on the long journey from Africa, and it's a yam that's growing in that garden. No matter what they say, everybody still calls it the sweet potato patch.

People have been makin' moonshine for as long as they've been here, but it was Elijah who'd revealed what was to come when he said, "The Spirit told me that 'the yam spirits will save the island.'"

"What's 'the yam spirits'?" I asked.

"You know, moonshine… made from the yams."

"You sure it didn't say 'the damn spirits'?"

"No, the Spirit don't do all that cursing. It said, 'the *yam* spirits.'"

"And you're sure that's what it meant?" I asked.

"What else could it mean? You think some yam ghosts are gonna save the island? You don't have to listen if you don't want to. I'm just tellin' you what The Spirit told me, and it told me that 'the yam spirits will save the island.'"

We started out with *Yam Bam Beer* and then *Yam Bam Whisky.* Before we knew it, the women were gatherin' in the Community Center makin' *Yam Bam Pies* and *Yam Bam Molasses* and *Yam Bam Candy.* Chefs from the mainland started buying our whisky to use in their desserts, ice cream and cakes covered with caramel whisky sauce and whisky cream. Then they started using it to glaze ribs and pork loins and mix into black currant sauce drizzled over top of roast grouse. They made whisky bread and whisky marmalade.

Word musta' got out, and Roger Kellogg, a filmmaker with the PBS *Southern Lens* series contacted us wantin' to make a documentary. The elders met and discussed it, and we decided that the more attention we can draw to our situation and the injustices that are happening every day as we are being forced off our land, the better.

I really didn't have time for this foolishness, but there was no gettin' rid of these two. They was all worked up. "Get on that side of the bed and grab that sheet. Remember how I showed you how to make the hospital corners?" Jasmine was too wrapped up in her story to pay any attention. "De'Andre, grab that sheet and pull it tight." De'Andre grabbed the sheet and jerked it so hard it came clear off the bed and flew up on the ceiling fan. I stopped and looked him dead in the eye, and that's when I knew something was wrong, bad wrong.

As if enunciating each syllable, "GRAND-MA, THERE. IS. A. DEAD. WO-MAN. IN. THE. SWEET. PO-TA-TO. PATCH," and then the room went silent, and even Jasmine was still.

"*Who* is in the sweet potato patch?" They looked at each other 'cause they know you ain't supposed to speak the name of the dead. "I said, *who* is in the sweet potato patch?"

"Miss Maya."

I let the weight of their words settle in my chest. "Wait here."

I walked to the cottage where Maya had been staying, and eased the door open. Sure enough, Maya's bags were still there at the foot of the bed. She had been scheduled to take the nine o'clock ferry back to the mainland. I picked up the phone and rang Jed.

"Jed, did you take Maya to the dock this mornin'?"

"Well, I came to get her 'round half past eight, but she wasn't there. I looked around and waited for 'bout fifteen or twenty minutes. I reckoned she musta decided to stay a li'l longer so I went back home."

"Jed, I think there's a problem. Come pick me up. I'll be waitin' at The Sandbar."

Jed owned the Sandbar, but I knew where he kept the key, and I took advantage of the few minutes to go inside and help myself to a shot of whisky to calm my nerves. We drove to the cut and parked the truck off to the side of the main road and got out and walked to the sweet potato patch. The second we opened the door to the truck I smelled it, just like Blue's mule, somethin' was dead. The buzzards knew it too, but they hadn't come down yet. They was up in the trees waitin', so I knew it hadn't been too long. Jed pulled two handkerchiefs outta nowhere.

"Here," he said, "tie this 'round your face."

I did just as he had done, coverin' my mouth and nose. I could see a body propped up against the far end of the garden, and that was close enough for me. "Her spirit can't be too far above her head, and I'm not messin' with no spirit." Jed stopped, too. In an instant, I felt like I knew nothin', like I had never known nothin' in my whole life, nothin' about nothin', 'cause this didn't fit anything I knew or had ever known. "This doesn't make any sense, Jed."

He walked a little closer, turning back to look at me, and as if to save me from myself he said, "Stay here." I looked down at my feet, and they couldn't move even if I had wanted them to, like all the roots of all the sweet potatoes had anchored to my feet, and they just wouldn't let me go no farther. Jed took a few more steps and stopped about ten feet from the body. After a few minutes he turned and walked back to where my feet was stuck to the ground.

"Is she dead?" Without saying a word, he shook his head and led the way back to his truck. At last my feet could move, but I swear I could feel her spirit. I kept turning and looking over my shoulder, but no matter which way I turned I could feel every hair standing up on my neck and head, like she was right behind me.

Jed cranked up the truck and I jumped in the passenger side, and we headed for the GIPS's office. "You call the elders, and I'll go pick up Miss Althea and Vernon. Don't tell 'em what happened, just tell 'em to be at the Community Center in fifteen minutes, and call Tobias too."

"But Tobias ain't an el…"

"I know. Call Tobias. He needs to be there." I knew what he meant, even though I didn't agree with him hearin' the news like that.

As soon as I finished makin' the calls I headed down the dirt road to the center. It wasn't 'til I stepped inside and looked at the tables set up with table cloths and fresh cut flowers that it hit me—here we had film makers comin' all the way from Alabama, already on their way, and chefs coming from the mainland to celebrate the yam, and we had a dead sister in the sweet potato patch, and not just any sister, a white sister, a dead white sister in the sweet potato patch. The documentary was the least of our worries.

The elders arrived, nineteen of them total, eight men and eleven women, plus me and Jed made twenty-one, and Tobias made twenty-two. You woulda thought it was a family reunion the way they was all carryin' on, huggin' and tellin' jokes, like we don't all live on the same three-mile stretch of land. The bass in Jedidiah's voice and the grave expression on his face got everyone's attention.

"We got a problem. Some of you know one of the Soul Sisters who's been comin' here for years to help with the Cultural Celebration Day and the sweet potato garden, the white woman, Maya.

Gerald, who was already drunk by ten o'clock in the mornin', raised his hand, "That big bootied white woman?" The room started buzzin'.

Jedidiah's words caught in his throat, and with a slight cough he replied, "Yep, that's the one." He paused, lookin' around the room until he had everyone's full attention. "She's in the sweet potato patch."

Gerald raised his hand again, "Ooo, she wearin' them runnin' shorts with the snake boots again?"

"Ummmm, I uhhh, I don't know. She's in the sweet potato patch, but she's dead. She is laid up 'gainst a tree, and she is dead as she can be." Lord, everybody started talkin' all at once, 'cept for Gerald who started cryin' a little.

I looked at Tobias to see his reaction. I saw his jaws clench and his arms tighten across his chest, and he stared at the floor.

Solomon spoke up next, "You mean there's a dead

white woman in the sweet potato patch? How she die, in *our* sweet potato patch?"

"I don't know, but it looks like she got beat, real bad." Still eyeing Tobias, I saw nothin', no reaction. He certainly had reason to kill her after the way she had done him. Everybody was talkin' and carryin' on.

"There ain't no way one of our people did that. No way. We been here for over two hundred years and ain't nothin' like this ever happen. Them white women ain't nothin' but trouble, and that's what this gonna be. Trouble," Phillip said.

"They ain't never gonna believe a white person kill another white person."

The elders went back and forth 'bout what to do 'bout it. Everybody had an opinion 'cept for Tobias, who remained silent the whole time.

I kept waitin' for Elijah to say what he was really thinkin', what we was all thinkin'. "I knew once all these white folks started comin' to our island somethin' like this would happen. And what you thinks gonna happen when the police get here and see a dead white woman on Goethe? They gonna hang us from our own trees. That's what they gonna do." He cut his eyes towards Tobias. "Hail don't fall on just one roof, ya' know. We all guilty now. Shit, makes me wanna kill 'er again."

Jedidiah went on, "There's another problem." Everybody got quiet again. "We got folks comin' from the mainland on the next ferry over to make a documentary about the property taxes and *Yam Bam Spirits*. This was supposed to be some big publicity for us, raise awareness, and we can't have no dead woman in the sweet potato patch. That just won't work. That ain't the kinda publicity we lookin' for. We gotta get that woman outta here."

James raised his hand, like we was in school or somethin'. "If you got a dead white woman that's been murdered, that's gonna be one angry spirit. You gots to take the body 'round the island, let her spirit find who did it, and when she find who did it, then she only gonna mess wid' that person, and she leave the rest of us alone. If you just leave her in the sweet potato patch, and she ain't got no chance to accuse no one, then she gonna be callin' our grandkids' names and tryin' to take 'em wid' her. You know how much that woman loved Jasmine. She be callin' Jasmine's name at night, and you know Jazz so curious, she'd fall for it every time. I say you gotta get that body and drive it all over da island. Then you get rid of her."

"Get rid of her? Where she gonna go?" Livie asked. "We on an island. There ain't nowhere for her to go, and we all know ain't no one gonna touch no dead body. God bless the dead."

Jesup chimed in, "You ever read *Native Son* by Richard Wright? 'Member how Bigger Thomas cut that white woman's body up and burned it in the furnace?" That made Livie hot, and the two of them went back and forth for some time.

"Ain't nobody gonna touch that woman, much less cut her up and burn her in a furnace. That's just crazy."

"Why you think he did that? He knew what was gonna happen he got caught with a dead white woman's body, so he cut her up, got rid of her. What you think's gonna happen to us?"

"Well you ain't no Bigger Thomas. 'Member when you couldn't even put down that rabid raccoon? Who had to come shoot it for you? Who? Me, that's who, and I ain't cutting up no dead body for you!"

"We got a whole ocean full a hungry fish and sharks. Let's just tie her to somethin' heavy, take that body out and dump that thing."

"That body'd be washin' up on the beach with cinder blocks tied 'round its neck just like Dare Devil. Wouldn't that be somethin'?"

Dare Devil was Moses Wright's dog. That thing slept in the middle of the road its whole life, which turned out to be 'bout eight years, and everybody knew to drive 'round it 'til one day Gerald, who'd had a few too many, hit that thing like a speed bump, killin' it dead. In his drunken stupor it made perfect sense to Gerald to "borrow" Reginald's boat to give Dare Devil a proper burial at sea so that no one would ever have to know. Gerald tied a cinder block 'round Dare Devil's neck, said a prayer and commenced singin' "His eye is on the sparrow, and I know he watches me." The irony being, His eye mighta been on the sparrow, but it wasn't on the dog. Jesus was sure not watchin' out for Dare Devil that day, and he wasn't lookin' out for Gerald the next day neither when the current caught that dog and washed it right up on the beach where some USCB kids was playin'. They ran straight to Moses tellin' him someone had murdered his dog. Gerald had to come clean 'bout the whole thing, and neither Moses nor Reginald would talk to him for 'bout a year. It became a joke among the rest of us when someone was crackin' wise with you to say to that person, "Hey, you remember what happened to Dare Devil…"

"She got a family. It ain't like they ain't gonna come lookin' for her."

"This is Goethe. It's wild out here. Anything coulda

happened to her."

"She coulda fell into a wood chipper."

"What the hell a white woman gonna be chippin' wood on Goethe for?"

"It ain't like she's the only white person who's ever been here. Where would it make sense to find a white woman? Not chippin' wood and not in the sweet potato patch. That's for sure."

"You got all the university students down on the north end."

"How you gonna sneak a body in the middle of a bunch of college kids?"

"The mansion. Take her to the mansion." Everyone got quiet because we all knew that was the most logical place for a white woman to be.

"Now that's the first thing you said that made any sense."

Henry Colleton had bought the whole south end of the island in 1807 and built a mansion with fifteen bedrooms and ten bathrooms, purchasing five hundred slaves to work the land. The DNR (Department of Natural Resources) owns the mansion now, and it has become a popular tourists' destination, especially for white folks. They'd come in droves, rent the place out for themselves and thirty of their closest friends. The descendants, on the other hand, avoided the mansion as a matter of principle.

Elanda knew Maya better than any of us because she was Jasmine's grandma, and every time Maya would come to the island Jasmine would hear that her "sista" was there, and she'd bug Elanda to take her over to The Cottages. Maya always brought something special from the mainland for her, a bracelet, a sewing kit, a book, something.

"She ain't never go to the mansion," Elanda said.

"They don't know that. All I'm saying is, it makes sense. She's white and white people usually wanna go see the mansion, take a tour or something. How many white people you see workin' in the sweet potato patch? Nobody gonna think twice 'bout a white woman at the mansion," Livie said.

It made sense. Problem was, ain't nobody wanna touch her, which started the whole debate 'bout who would move the body out of the sweet potato patch. At first they said Jedidiah 'cause he called the meeting, then Elias, 'cause he was the President of GIPS, only Elias was in Charleston and wouldn't be back for a few days. Then they talked 'bout drawin' lots.

This kinda talk went on for another half hour when Tobias spoke up for the first time. "I'll take care of her." Everyone stopped talkin' and watched him as he turned and walked out, got in his truck and drove off towards the sweet potato patch.

I was a poor boy, Papa, when you decided you would make me wealthy. I had the sickness in my bones. I was sure enough far from home. You made me healthy. I was rejected, dejected, uncorrected, unprotected, defeated from my people. I was contriving, cliff diving, capsizing, no freedom rising from that deep hole, but you made me free, and I must sing. You baptized me, just doin' your thing.

- Josh Garrels

3

Tobias

I pulled my truck down the cut, far as I could go, got out and closed the door softly. Lettin' the tailgate down, I climbed in the back and lit up a cigarette, wishin' I had something stronger than tobacco. Suckin' in the sweet smoke, I let it fill every inch of my lungs, holdin' it as long as I could before lettin' it out. I could see her across the garden, laid up 'gainst a tree, just like they said. I musta' smoked at least four, five cigarettes 'fore I got up the nerve to even think 'bout goin' over to where she was.

It had been almost seven years since I first laid eyes on her. The bluefish had been runnin', and I had been fishin' off the dock when the mornin' ferry came over from the mainland. Everybody got off the ferry like they do, and it's hard not to notice a white woman. Everybody loaded up in the back of the trucks and headed inland, 'cept for her. Clearly she had never been to Goethe before, and she didn't know what to do. She stood 'round in the parking lot for 'bout five minutes, like she was waitin' on some kind of shuttle service. I just kept fishin'. I knew better than to mess with some white woman, and it wasn't my problem if she didn't have a ride. Eventually she wandered down to where I was and set down 'side me.

"Any luck?" I looked at her, the first real look I had gotten. She was beautiful, different. Her hair, the color of corn silk, unfurled into waves that hung halfway down her back. She pulled her hair to the side. Her earrings, cowry shells surrounded by colorful beads, showed off her long thin neck and collarbones like white women in magazine ads. She wore a thin loose skirt that hugged the outline of her thick hips and thighs, accentuating her small waistline. Everything about her a combination of kept and unkept, beautiful and strange.

Her toenails, freshly painted, the same color blue as Mrs. Hattie's prized orchid she'd picked up from Lowe's on the mainland, didn't match anything that she wore. If she hadn't been wearing flip-flops I'd have sworn she didn't own a pair of shoes. Her feet were dirty, her heals dry and cracked, like she'd gone barefoot all summer. She swung her feet back and forth over the water, makin' unnecessary noises with her flip-flops as they slapped the bottoms of her feet and occasionally dipped into the water. She laid back on the dock, closin' her eyes and stretchin' her arms out above her head as her shirt climbed higher, revealin' the creamy white skin of her stomach. I sat on my bucket thinkin' about all the fish guts and spoiled bait that littered the dock on a regular basis that somehow didn't cause her a moment's hesitation. It wasn't her body that caught my attention. It was her T-shirt. As much as I wanted to put her on the first ferry back to the mainland, part of me was relieved to know that it wouldn't be returnin' for another eight hours, and I welcomed the distraction. At least she was interestin', a beautiful surprise.

I was born on Goethe, lived my whole life on the island, and just like most kids who grow up here I couldn't wait to get away. I spent all of my middle school and high school years playing football and baseball on the mainland, praying for a scholarship, only there weren't many scouts coming to Dale to check out the local talent, but God had me. I was accepted to Louisiana State University with a chance to walk on the baseball team my freshman year.

After proving myself on the field and in the classroom, the coach came to me and offered me a scholarship as long as I kept my GPA above a 2.7 and kept the grounders from getting past my position in the infield. There it was, her purple T-shirt with "Geaux Tigers!" the official LSU lettering. My alma mater. The place where I learned a little more about who I was in the world, where I made love to more women than I'd want to admit to, where I played and prayed, studied hard and cheated even harder, where some of the craziest, most carefree, fun times of my life happened. Baton Rouge. Ten and a half hours away, and here she was wearing an LSU shirt. LSU.

I didn't say nothin'. I started reelin' in my line. She sat up. "What you fishin' for?" I held my words behind my teeth. Thank goodness somethin' grabbed my line just then and started pullin' hard. I jerked my rod to set the hook and started reelin' it in. She kept talkin' and askin' questions, and I kept ignorin' her.

I finally stopped reelin' and turned to look at her as if to say, "Can't you see you the only one talkin'?" There was somethin' about her eyes, her expression, her smile, her excitement over everything and nothin'. She seemed so innocent, so full of life, so naïve. There was somethin' pure about her, pure and sweet like sugar. In that one look I was reminded of what it felt like to be a kid on Goethe. What it felt like when life was simple, when I still believed that stars were just old starfish shinin' on heaven's shores.

My son used to say, "That makes me feel like mornin'."

One day I asked him, "Whatcha mean by that?"

"You know, when you wake up early in the mornin', and you can't wait to get outta' bed just so you can see what's gonna happen that day?"

A question. Like he wasn't sure if I had ever known what that felt like or not. He saw the stress of debt on me, a big house, two luxury cars, a boat, a motorcycle, a full time job and a full time hustle. It's a lot simpler to have nothing, but my time on the mainland lured me in. Torn between two worlds, I was tired of being a victim of my choices.

Goethe's different. Things don't matter on Goethe. You don't need nothin'. You spend part a your day fishin' or crabbin' so you got something to eat, and that's all you need. You pull up in your yard and tell your cousin to start the fire while you go get the oysters. You come back to a yard full a folks, and you spend the rest of the night hangin' by the fire, laughin' and shuckin' oysters, eatin' like kings.

I thought about what he said for a minute. "Morning. Yeah, I remember that feelin'. It's just been a long time, too long."

She looked like she might feel like mornin' all day long, and I swore I would not look at her again. I kept reel-ing in my line, kept ignoring her. Finally, I reeled in my first bluefish of the season and realized I'd left my pliers in the truck. I thought about cuttin' the line, but something, maybe fate, made me say, "Hey, can you just put your foot right here? I gotta go get my pliers outta' the truck. Don't let it go now." Those were supposed to be my first and last words to her. I ran to the truck, grabbed my pliers and ran back to the dock. I couldn't a been gone more than two minutes, and there she was, blood runnin' down her arm, and she was squeezin' one hand tight as she could with the other.

"Jesus, I told you to put your foot on it, not stick your hand in its mouth." I didn't have nothin' to worry 'bout 'cause this one wasn't gonna last one night on the island. I grabbed my knife and cut the line and threw my only catch back in the water, and washed my hands off. She was still standin' there. "Come here. Let me see it." She walked over, clearly mad, tears welled up in her eyes, blue eyes the color of cotton candy after a greedy child has taken a slobbery bite, leavin' behind a darker blue outer edge. Between cursin', bitin' her lip, and suckin' in deep breaths, her exasperation made me smile.

"Open your hand." She slowly unclenched her fist, and I took her hand to examine it. I opened a bottle of water and let it pour over her fingers, revealin' a few little loose flaps of skin. I took out my handkerchief and wrapped it tight 'round her hand. "Nothin' a little Superglue can't fix." Then I threw my baitfish in the water, and packed up my tackle box and rod and reel. I stopped and looked at her, again. Retardedly irresistible. I couldn't just leave her there. "Come on." That was the first time I ever took a white woman home.

I put out my cigarette, and walked over to where she was. The closer I got the more my heart welled up in my chest. How did she always manage to do this to me, to make me feel so much? I learned long ago to not let my heart control my mind, otherwise I mighta' gone crazy. There had been too much pain and too much loss to feel anymore. I learned that to survive that kinda' pain my mind had to be stronger than my heart.

It took almost two years, but somehow she wore down my resolve to never let anyone in again. I knew early on that she had something that I wanted. I longed for that time in my life before I had lost the four cornerstones—both of my parents, my brother, and my only son. I wanted to go back to that time when I believed that life was good and full of hope. Every time she came to the island I found her. I'd teach her how to fish, how to crab, how to dig for clams, how to harvest oysters and throw a cast net, anything I could think of to see her, to know her.

At night I'd look for the bonfire, and I'd find her there, dancing away with my heart. I'd show up, like I was just there. She didn't know I never went out unless she was on the island. She'd feel me walk in every time, like our souls were connected, and she'd stare at me shamelessly, like everyone wasn't talkin', like she didn't have a care in the world, like I was the only man there, the only man on the island. She'd come over after a while and without a word she'd take me by the hand leading me to the makeshift dance floor on the porch, and I'd show her how a brother does it, pressing up against her, finding our rhythm. Minutes melted into hours, until I'd begin to think of my wife. A sobering combination of bitterness and guilt would overtake me, and I'd go sit by the fire, far enough away to relieve my conscience and still close enough to feel her.

She'd follow behind me. She is white, and I am from Goethe. I'd made enough mistakes in my life, and I was determined that she wouldn't be the next. I sat back in the old folding chair, no empty seat next to me. She didn't hesitate, walking around to the other side of the fire pit, settling in beside Elanda who was always crocheting a blanket for one of the grandkids. I'd try not to look, not to think of her, wishing she hadn't followed me. I'd watch Elanda pass her the blanket, and she'd take over crocheting line after line as they laughed. She'd never even look up. After a while the crowd would thin out. Elanda would take her blanket and go home.

I close my eyes, taking me back as I imagine it's just us sitting by the fire again. I lean back in my seat, locking my eyes on hers, silently wondering if this could ever really happen. Without a sound she makes the first move, walking away. I watch, her hips swaying in time with every rhythm of every desire I've ever known, as she wanders around the yard. She finds a stick and brings it to where I am. She bends down beside me.

"How many kids you say you got, and how old are they?" She uses the stick to begin drawing a family tree in a patch of sand where the grass refuses to grow.

I laugh, "You gonna need more sand than that. We might have to go down to the beach at *low tide* for you to have enough room." I can't think of a better way to scare her off except maybe the details of my child support.

Without hesitation she says, "Let's go."

"Go where?"

"To the beach. It's low tide," and with that she climbs on the back of my motorcycle with me still standing there. She pats the seat in front of her. "Well, come on. Let's go." I sigh, shaking my head and smiling. She makes me feel like mornin'.

It wasn't like me to be led around by some woman, but who was I kidding? She'd been leading me around since that first day at the dock. I try not to smile too big as I climb on, and she wraps her body against mine so tight I feel like she's melting into me, and I wonder why I haven't taken her for a ride before. She probably thinks the island is much bigger than it actually is because I manage to ride around it three times before finally making it to the beach. Sure enough, she finds a stick and maps out the story of my life, women from New York to Louisiana, daughters spread everywhere in between. She stops drawing and looks at me, looks back at the map of my life and back to me.

"What?"

She laughs, "I see how you ended up with so many kids."

"What you mean?"

She smiles, "I mean, you're an amazing man. You're beautiful, passionate, hard working, fun." She almost says it. She almost opens the door.

There had been many women who wanted all kinds of things from me, but she was the first woman I can ever recall who wanted my heart, and she chased it relentlessly, digging deeper and deeper with every question. My soul had been shattered into pieces, leaving sharp jagged edges that threatened to cut anyone who came too close, but she held them fearlessly, carefully laying them out next to the debris of her own soul, smoothing out the roughness. They fit together easily, forming a mesmerizing mosaic, and for the first time I could see beauty in the brokenness and purpose in the pain.

She started to wake somethin' up inside of me, wearin' me down. My heart and my mind were doin' rounds, and my heart was winnin'. I'd tell myself that I wouldn't see her the next time she came to the island, but she was somehow part of me, like a bad habit I didn't want to break, like the first hit of nicotine when you wake up.

"Look. There. In the edge of the water!" she points. I am scared of the ocean, especially at night, and by her excitement I think it might be a shark. She takes me by the hand, running for the water. It would be like her to run towards a shark with wild wonder and take me with her. "Do you see that? What is it?" The shoreline glows and small fish zip through the water like lightning, disappearing into the deep.

"That's bioluminescent plankton."

"Bio- what?" she asks, running her foot across the wet sand leaving behind a trail of shooting stars that quickly disappear.

"Bioluminescent plankton. They're little creatures that light up." I stand still, watching as she shuffles her feet backwards, moonwalking across the sand and water, admiring the mini universe at the mercy of her toes.

"Look! It's like I have sparklers attached to my feet!"

I laugh, "I think you're killin' 'em." She jumps up and down until suddenly, as if they can communicate with each other, they light up all at once for a split second. In that moment the whole universe is magically hers, and then just like that they are gone, nothing but a memory. She has an unquenchable curiosity to know about things, history, nature, people, the world. There are parts of her that remind me of who I used to be.

Then, without a word, she pulls her shirt up over her head, dropping it to the sand, slides her skirt down over her hips, and is standing there in bra and panties, no different than a bathing suit, but I'm not sure if I'm supposed to turn around or get naked. With any other woman this can only mean one thing, but I am just as confused as I am aroused. And then she runs into the ocean. Alone. At night. It is like she is drunk. *All of the time.* I laugh, and then minutes later she is standing in front of me, soaking wet and cold, shaking. Laughing, she grabs me in a tight hug, like she expects me to push her away to keep myself from getting wet, but I can't. She lets go and tells me to turn around.

"Hold this." She slings her wet bra across my shoulder and then her panties. Thinking to myself, "How fast can I get naked? I'll take her up to the picnic tables at the pavilion. There won't be much sand there. "Okay, you can turn around now."

"You're dressed!?!"

She laughs. "Yeah, what'd you think?" She takes her bra and panties from my hands. "Thanks. I didn't want to get sand all over them."

Wildly innocent. That's what she was. Not a tease. Just pure. Carefree. The kind of woman who'd ride with the windows down, dance in the rain and bring home stray animals.

I wasn't sure which was worse, seeing her soaking

wet in bra and panties or feeling the warmth of her body wrapped around mine knowing she didn't have on either under her clothes. She simply drove me crazy, and she didn't even know it.

I began to want her, to think of her when she was gone, to imagine what it would be like to kiss her, to hold her, to wake up next to her. At first her eyes. Then her smile. Her mouth. Her neck. Her breasts. I imagined the curve of her waist that led to those hips and thighs. Her calves. Her toes. I wanted all of her, more than she knew, more than she would ever know. I never kissed her, never told her how I felt. After a drink or two I'd head home alone. The next day I'd just happen to ride by her cottage as she was wandering outside, headed to the beach with her coffee, and I'd offer her a ride like I had been headed that way all along.

She talked unlike anyone I'd ever met before. There wasn't nothin' she wouldn't say. I don't think she'd ever had a thought cross her mind that didn't come outta her mouth. I was just the opposite. She poured her heart out, whether I wanted to hear it or not, which I did.

"We got married too young," she said. "It feels like being lost in the desert for fifteen years, my eyes stinging, my skin dry like a wheat field, stained from years and layers of dirt, red clay and sand so that I can hardly recognize myself anymore. He chose the family business over me again and again. He didn't take care of me."

She was broken. In another life she would have been nothing more than easy prey, vulnerable, but she was becoming more than that to me. "I want to bring rain to your life. I want to watch you heal and lead you out of the desert and into the Promised Land." What I really wanted was her.

"I don't need anyone to rescue me," she said. The more I got to know her, the more I realized that it wasn't weakness that made her vulnerable. She was stronger than I knew. I could put my emotions in a box that I kept locked, but she felt everything. I just happened to come into her life at the right time, and just like me, she was drawn back again and again.

I never spoke her name, like it was sacred, and it didn't occur to me that she never spoke my name either until I heard her say it. "Tobias, 'the goodness of God.' That's what your name means. Did you know that?" I shook my head. "That's what I see in you. God's goodness." To this day that's the only time I can remember her calling me by my name.

I had made so many mistakes. There was a long history with women on and off the island. I could have, and did have, any woman on the island I wanted, any woman who came to the island, except for her. She was off limits, and maybe that was part of it. I'd never met anyone who could hold my attention or my heart. I was older now, and ready for something more. She knew about all of the women. Sisters on the island talk, but still all she could see was the goodness of God.

"Love is blind, ya' know?" I said.

"That's not true. It just sees more."

"If you like my name so much, why you call me TK? I mean, I know it's my initials, but you the only one who ever called me that."

"'Cause it sounds like 'Tea Cake.'"

"Well, I am pretty sweet, aren't I?"

She laughed, "I mean *Their Eyes Were Watching God.*"

"Zora Neale Hurston. Honestly, I'm embarrassed to admit I've never read it."

"Tea Cake is one of the main characters, and you remind me of him." She paused, looking at me. "There's a movie," and with that she smiled.

That night I took my laptop and sat out on the porch of the library, the only spot on the island with Wi-Fi, and I watched the whole movie, and that was the first time that I knew it wasn't just me. It wasn't just in my head.

I had never trusted anyone with my heart, but she shared hers again and again with that same openness. Somehow this woman I thought wouldn't make it a day on Goethe had possessed the strength to anchor the seas of my soul. I had been avoiding the hard decisions and just letting things go for so long.

"I got married for the second time eight years ago, but it was a mistake from the start. She hates the island, hates nature, hates the simplicity of life here. We're so different I can't even remember why we got married. She likes to shop, eat in fancy restaurants, and drive a Lexus. About two years ago she found a job in Charleston and left, just like that. She comes home about once a month for the weekend, and we fight the whole time, and I'm so glad when she finally leaves. I learned to settle and stop believing that life could be different, that it could be better."

Still being married, that was all I could say. I couldn't tell Maya that every time she came to the island I found myself letting her weave her heart into mine, and every time she left I realized she was taking another piece of me back to the mainland. I'd be alright when I didn't see her, but then she'd return with my heart, making me whole again, and I'd realize how lost I had been without her. Feeling complete only made me realize what life could be like, what it should be like, and then she'd leave again, and I'd be alright 'til the next time.

Once she came to Goethe just for the day. I picked her up at the ferry and took her out to the campgrounds to throw the cast net in the folly. We threw for about a half hour. She was quiet. I could feel her nervousness making my heart race. She held the net in her hands and paced back and forth in the edge of the sand. Something was different, wrong. There was an undeniable tension, and it scared me.

I couldn't take it. Finally I asked, "What's wrong?" She turned and looked at me and shook her head. She was holding back, and I couldn't understand why because that was something she never did. Her cheeks blushed and she bent over with her hands on her knees to catch her breath.

"Maya, what's going on? Tell me." She stood, took one look at me and went back to pacing. "Maya, tell me. Just say it. Whatever it is, just say it." My heart was about to come through my chest. Taking her by the shoulders, I thought I might shake her. She looked like she was about to cry, and I knew something was wrong.

"I have a crush on you, and it's got me all messed up. You're all I can think about, and you've already been married, what, three times?"

"Twice. TWICE. I've only been married *twice*."

"Oh, thank God, 'cause I seriously think I might be in love with you, and I could *not* be wife number four," she laughed nervously, and it made me smile.

She had said it. She spoke what I had been feeling all along. She had opened that door, and there was no going back.

"Yeah, well you got my head spinnin' every time you come 'round. I can't think straight just knowing you're on the island." It was the first I had ever let her know with words how she affected me.

She looked relieved for a second. She smiled. She smiled with her eyes and her mouth and her whole body. It was hard to imagine having the power to make someone that happy. "I can't look at you right now," she said, dropping her net and making her way about a tenth of a mile through the marsh and grass to sit on an old driftwood tree. I smiled, my mind racing, and threw the cast net about a half a dozen times to clear my head before following her. She really couldn't look at me. I thought she might take off through the marsh again, but I caught her by the hand, the same hand I had first held and cared for years before.

"I want to kiss you so bad right now," I said.

"You can *not* kiss me."

"Why not?"

"I'm scared."

"Of what? That you might kiss me back?"

She smiled and said, "That I might throw up." I laughed. I'd never had a woman tell me that she might throw up if I kissed her.

"You already said you'd marry me." I took a step towards her, and she didn't run away. I kissed her for the first time. It was just like I'd imagined, innocent and pure. Afterwards she grabbed me and hugged me so close I could feel her heart beating against my chest, and she wouldn't let go.

Finally I said, "You gonna throw up?"
She laughed, "Maybe."

Our souls had become so intertwined over the years it was like half of me was laid up 'gainst that tree. What in the world had happened? I knew, like the elders said, that none of my people had anything to do with this. As much as they wanted white people off the island, our strategy had been to remain invisible for as long as possible, not to kill anyone. Goethe was the most peaceful place I'd ever known. It didn't fit, didn't make any sense.

I put out my last cigarette and exhaled, knowing at some point I had to take care of her body. I hated seeing her like this and tried to imagine her as she had been on that first day at the dock. Finally, I made a decision that I would just do it. I would just pick her up and move her to the back of my truck. There was no more waiting. Scooping her up into my arms, keeping my eyes straight ahead to the bed of my truck, and refusing to look down at her, I slid her in the back and turned quickly to walk away. "Breathe. Breathe. Breathe. Just keep breathing. You can do this." Why had I smoked every last cigarette?

Walking to the edge of the sweet potato patch, I gathered some moss and wildflowers. I returned to the truck and tucked the moss under her head and laid the flowers on her body. Even though I knew they'd probably blow out on the ride, it still seemed like the right thing to do, and that's when I saw it, the note, clutched in her hand. I didn't have to read it. I knew what it said. I had told her to bury it. Never asking where she'd put it, I assumed she would have taken it to the mainland where she could get to it. I should have known she had put it in the sweet potato patch.

I walked over to the spot, and sure enough there was a deep hole with a conch shell beside it. I debated taking the note and reburying it, but she had died with it in her hand. It had been that important to her, and I couldn't do it. I couldn't take it from her. I just couldn't. My name wasn't on it, so I let it be. I threw the shell in the hole and kicked the dirt back in until it was completely covered. I walked over to the tree where she had been. Just like I thought, there was a Tupperware container and small backpack with an iPhone and a small Nalgene bottle, which I could only assume had moonshine in it. I threw it all in her backpack and placed it beside her in the truck.

Putting up the tailgate so no one would see, I set off to ride her 'round the island so her spirit could find who had done this to her. Crazy as it sounded, I grew up on Goethe, and even though I'd left the island for years, gone off to college, I found my way back because there were parts of Goethe that get inside of you, and you can't get 'em out no matter how much you learn about the world. Goethe becomes the only place that makes any sense. We were all brought up bein' told 'bout spirits and how to care for the dead. If she had been black, been from Goethe, this woulda' all been very different. Everybody'd be takin' care of her spirit, sendin' her on her way back to Africa. They'd be putting food and money in her windowsill. They'd mourn for days and throw a big funeral. Everyone would take part, knowin' that when they got to heaven she'd be there waitin', and in the meantime her spirit would be lookin' out for those who'd taken care to send her on her way. But she was white, and this was Goethe.

I spent the next thirty minutes riding 'round the

island, down every dirt road, past the DNR office, past the USCB dorms, down by the beach, past Canaan Cemetery, 'round by the old church, and out to the mansion. The mansion was now owned by the DNR, which had a group of men who did maintenance on the property all day long. Fortunately, they had gone on a late lunch. They'd be back soon, and once they found her they'd make the call to the Sheriff's Department. I wasn't sure how I felt about leaving her at the mansion. Just like the descendants, she had adopted the notion of staying away because of all it stood for. She never came to Goethe to live it up as if she had her own private island. She came to Goethe because she loved the wildness of it, loved the adventure, loved nature, loved the people, loved the history, loved the simplicity. As far as I knew she'd never been to the mansion 'cept for passing by it on the way to the beach.

I pulled my truck in front, as close as I could to the swimming pool. It didn't have any water in it. It never did. I don't know why. I imagined the pool to be like God's hands cupped together, surrounded by giant moss covered live oaks that would give her shade. Carrying her body down the steps of the pool, I laid her down in God's hands. That's where I had to leave her. I pulled out my cell phone and opened a compass app, making sure her body was facing east. I ran back to my truck and grabbed her bag, the moss and all the flowers that were left. Anxious to get out of there before the workers came back, I pushed the moss up under her head, scattered the flowers across her chest and set down her bag. I reached in my pocket for some change, placing a quarter over each of her eyes, then ran back to my truck.

Not wanting to be seen heading away from the

mansion, I drove on down to the beach, just a quarter mile away. As much as I loved the beach, I hated going in the water. To tell you the truth, I was just scared, scared of all the things I couldn't see. Lots of people on Goethe are scared to swim in the ocean. Most folks will tell you it's 'cause our people were kidnapped from Africa and brought over on ships. We'll go in the ocean to drag the seine net, or out on the boat to fish, but we don't just go in the water for the heck of it. She had no reservations about swimming in the ocean, and I think she even liked knowing she could do something so easily that I wouldn't do. She told me once that she was born en caul, which meant when she came into this world, she was still hangin' out inside the amniotic sac. Doctors had heard about such births, but few of them had ever seen it. It was good luck and meant that she would never drown. I told her that didn't mean she wouldn't get eaten by a shark.

"What if I did get bit by a shark? Would you help me?"

"Yeah, I'd yell 'HEEEEELLLLLPP'!"

"This is Goethe. What if no one's around?"

"That's why you don't go swimming in the ocean."

"I'm gonna go swimming, and you should come with me. So, would you help me if I were dying in the ocean?"

"You're not going to die in the ocean. You were born en caul, remember? But I was not, which is why I'm gonna stay right here on the shore."

"But what if I did? What if I got a cramp or a jellyfish stung me? Maybe you're the one who saves me. Maybe you're part of the plan. Maybe you're the reason I don't drown."

Finally I'd relent. "Ok, I'd help you."

She'd smile and run into the ocean, but not before she'd add "One day you'll go swimming with me, and I'll save you too."

I pulled up to the pavilion and followed the boardwalk out to the beach. I stood there, imagining her running and jumping in the waves. I looked down the beach in both directions and no one was there. I stood at the edge of the water, and like her spirit had taken over me, I stripped off all my clothes, and walked into ocean to swim for the first time in my life.

Walls fall down. Where there's a peaceful sound, lonely souls hang around. Don't be shy. There's nothing left to hide. Come on let's talk a while of the places we left behind, no longer yours and mine. We could build a good thing here too. So give it just a little time. Share some bread and wine. Weave your heart into mine.

- Josh Garrels

4

Maya

My counselor peered at me from across the desk. "What would you say to the Israelites who had been in the desert for fifteen years, knowing they still had twenty-five years to go?" I eyed him curiously and cautiously. Levi and I had spent fifteen fruitless years in and out of counseling, when he was home. For years I had put my troubled heart, along with my trust in a group of men who ran the church. They were called and appointed to be elders for life. Unfortunately, the appointment outlasted the calling. They used their wisdom and discernment to determine that the problem lay solely in my heart, and in my attitude. "No one is ever promised happiness in this lifetime. True joy doesn't depend on your circumstances."

There were times that they read to us from *The Book of Extended Metaphors and Clichés for Troubled Marriages* with such inflection and intonation that I thought they might truly be able to exorcise the demons from our marriage and we would leave healed. Levi would get a job, and I could quit one of mine.

"Hand me the snake," I'd think to myself. "I'll dance with it. Dare me to drink the poison. After being trapped in a toxic marriage for fifteen years, to die is to gain." I drank the Kool-Aid, and their unwise counsel seeped just enough venom into the wounds so that I would waste away more quietly.

"You choose to focus on *your* needs and the things you *can't* have, rather than appreciating and nurturing the things you *do* have. What about your *husband's* needs?"

In reality, I could have named a hundred things that I wanted and needed, but they were all symptoms of the thing I wanted most, a husband who knew me, a husband who saw me, a husband who cared.

"You made a *commitment*, 'til death do you part.'"

As I desperately clawed my way through scorching sun and suffocating sand of the desert, they rested under the saving shade of a fan filled tent, sipping sweet tea and eating organic grapes, all the while urging me to pick myself up and run lest I die of exposure.

As always, I'd leave with a list of things to do: Read more. Pray more. Appreciate more. Love more. Believe more. So I prayed for death. I prayed for freedom. In another six months we would meet again for my venomous vaccine booster, and another six months and another six months, like being denied parole again and again.

After ten years of this, I knew that I didn't need counseling. I needed healing, and I needed absolution for what I was about to do. God was too far away to hear my prayers. This was my chance at a new beginning in a new location, and this counselor seemed different. Our marriage was a desert. That's all it had ever been. Just having someone recognize that, acknowledge it, and not pretend it had been some wonderful blessing that I failed to see, to have someone agree that it had been an arid wasteland, earned my trust and respect.

I thought about the question, "'What would I say to the Israelites?' You really want to know what I'd say? I'd say, 'Aren't you tired of this? Don't you ever wonder if there's something more?'"

"Even though they were in the desert, at least they were in God's will. God had them there for a reason. Do you still think they should leave?"

"If they were God's chosen people, and he's sovereign over all things, then if he allowed them to leave, wouldn't they still have been in his will? All I know is, I want more. I'm tired. I'm tired of this." I had already left the desert. Maybe I had even left God's will. I'm not sure. I would find my own way back to Eden, back to the Promised Land.

He heard me. He knew that I had come to him too late. My heart had been broken and scarred, and it had changed me. He just listened. And then he granted me parole, a free pass, a life sentence ended early. If I was God's, then he would never let me go. I was free.

We'd gotten married too young, when we were still in college. I was looking forward to teaching, blissfully unaware that all the things I wanted in a boyfriend would be vastly different than what I'd need in a husband and expect in a man.

"What did you love about him so much when you agreed to marry him?"

"He was passionate and adventurous. He didn't buy into social expectations and he was willing to take risks, but I didn't know that marrying someone with those qualities would mean that I would never get to be or do any of those things myself."

"What happened?"

"For graduation Levi's father bought him a plane ticket to Guyana, South America to mine for gold. His dad had quit his job, cashed in his 401Ks and decided to gamble all of his assets on the gold rush. He promised Levi big payouts if he went."

"What did you think about him leaving?"

"It seemed like perfect timing. Levi wasn't ready to cut his hair and take a job in the corporate world, but being a short order cook at a bar wasn't promising enough for me. I thought it would be good for him, for us, but once he left, it quickly became apparent that he'd also left the success and survival of our marriage up to me. He checked out."

"So what happened then?"

"Levi would come and go from Guyana, and I was left with the teaching career, which I truly did love. I just didn't know it would be the only thing that I would ever get to do. I carried his debts like an anchor tied around my neck. Fighting to tread water, taking care of all the bills, picking up side jobs, thinking for him. Eventually the weight of responsibility crushed me, binding my hands and dragging me under."

"What about when he came home?"

"That just meant more work. He came expecting a welcome home party, and dinner, and sex, and someone to listen to stories of giant excavators getting stuck in the mud, and heated negotiations with locals over land, and poisonous snakes and flecks of gold, but the truth was, I couldn't have cared less about any of it. I saw his eyes so full of life. I watched his lips move, but the words escaped me, like they were sucked straight into a giant vacuum and went some place where happy people live. They were wasted on me. Too tired to hear, my mind was heavy, filled up with thoughts of essays that I still hadn't gotten around to grading, the check that I needed to get in the mail before the water got turned off again, the empty coffee can. More than anything, I just needed rest, but he didn't seem to notice. Then he would leave, and the air would feel a little bit lighter, and I could breathe again."

"Did they ever find any gold?"

"Finally, after five years of coming and going, their site hit one point five million dollars in gold that summer. He called, and we celebrated over the phone, dreaming of all of the things we could do with the money, paying down debt, saving, spending, going on a real vacation together. I thought it had all been worth it; all the hard work, all of the sacrifice was finally going to pay off. I wouldn't have to clean houses on the weekends any more. I could pay off the car and replace the bald tires that were sure to send me hydroplaning across the highway after a light rain. I wouldn't have to sleep on the same mattress that I'd been sleeping on since I was ten, my ribs pressing into my lungs every morning. I thought things would finally change."

"So why didn't they?"

"By the time his dad went through the list of creditors, and paid back his own personal investments of 401Ks, equipment and plane tickets, Levi came home with one thousand dollar 'bonus,' mindless of the fact that he was rarely getting paid in the first place. I wanted so much to burn that bonus to show that it meant nothing to me, but instead I was reduced to a beggar who was thankful for a piece of stale, moldy bread. A thousand dollars was more help than I'd received in a long time. Desperate and needy, I took it and used it to pay bills."

"Did that wake Levi up?"

"He was proud to give me the money. He was hooked on the rush, explaining that now, with the company debt finally gone, and having learned so much, they'd hit it again, and then it would be our turn. Just like that, he was off to South America, mesmerized by the mirage."

"What about Fletch?"

"We had been married for three years when I got pregnant with Fletch, and I really thought that would change things, that he wouldn't be able to leave, that he would feel a sense of duty to stay home and get a normal job with a regular paycheck to provide for our family, but it only made him more determined to stay the course in Guyana, and we became worlds apart. He came and went for thirteen years, and I found myself a single mom trying to raise a man."

"That's a long time to live like that."

"It wasn't living. It was surviving. I learned how much my lungs loved the feel of oxygen. Every time he'd come home we'd fight until all the air was sucked from the room. By the time he'd leave I'd realize how much easier my life had become without him."

"So you moved here to start over, and that's when he came home, huh?"

"Yeah."

Hopeless and helpless, I lay among thousands in the Valley of Dry Bones, bones without tendons or flesh, without a pulse or breath, in between life and death. My heart physically ached to think of the dreams that would never come true, the passions I would never pursue, the way I would never be loved. Determined to stay the course, wanting to believe in God, a single verse from Proverbs captured my heart and described my angst. "A hope deferred makes the heart sick or dead, but a longing fulfilled is a tree of life." I longed for a lover I had never known and for a home where I had never lived. It seemed familiar, like a dream that I struggled to remember and at the same time couldn't forget. Everyone in the church said I had to die to myself in order to be free, but I had died a thousand deaths and still hadn't found freedom.

The year I taught 8th grade science I learned that the gravitational pull from the earth causes the moon to rotate at exactly the same rate at which it revolves around the earth, like two dancers, perfectly in sync. The result is that the same side of the moon always faces the earth, beautiful, dependable, predictable, even in its waxing and waning. I was the moon, pulled by the tide, waltzing my way through life. And just like the moon, I had a dark side, a side that was unknown, unexplored. I feared that someday I might bump into something or someone who could throw me out of my orbit and I'd go hurling, completely out of control through outer space.

Tired of clumsily waltzing my way around the dance floor with an imaginary partner, my heart was sick and dying. I read Langston Hughes again and again. I wanted to know his story, wanted to know his hopes and his longings, wanted to know if they were ever fulfilled or if he died waiting. Would I die waiting? How easily my disappointments had sugared over sweet as syrup for the first few years, and how bitter they had become over the decade that followed. I dreamed of a romantic picnic lunch with a dead poet.

"Mr. Hughes," I would say, "Tell me your story. Tell me what you've seen and suffered. They say some folks can carry more than others, but I'm done carrying this load. It's so heavy that I feel I might just lie down and never get back up. I'm so tired," and just then, my heart would explode, and Mr. Hughes and I would get sucked up into heaven through a tunnel of blue light, hand in hand, like old friends, he with his answers, and me, with freedom from my longing to be known and loved. I was ready for a new dance, something different. Maybe I'd learn how to do the tango or how to shag. Maybe I'd even twerk… in public.

And then it happened. My greatest hopes and fears collided in The Year of the Great Comet. His name was TK. We would meet on the dance floor, he doing the Cat Daddy and me waltzing all by myself, his catchy riff drowning out my elevator music, messing up my moves. Before I knew what had happened, there I was, standing in the middle of the dance floor, trying to remember my count, captivated by this celestial wonder, this beautiful surprise. It was there that I discovered a new rhythm, one that mysteriously matched the beat of my heart, releasing me from my orbit to spin and twirl and laugh and dance, really dance.

The problem is… after years in the valley, with lungs so completely depleted of oxygen, it's hard to tell the difference between life-giving air and poison gas. It all tastes and feels the same when you're just happy to breathe. So I leaned into the exhaust and sucked in the sweetness. Light-headed, the sky spinning in circles, I knew two things for certain: it might kill me, but I'd never felt more alive. Hooked, I went back for more again and again.

It had been years since I had been on vacation, years since I had been to the beach. I had spent most of my childhood at the coast, and I craved the water. I wanted to feel the hot sand on the bottoms of my feet as I ran as fast as I could into the cool salt water, letting it wash over me, healing my wounds, cleansing my soul, baptizing me. I wanted to believe that God was still good. I wanted it to be socially acceptable to walk around more naked than clothed. I wanted to drink a bottle of wine under a full moon until the stars spun like a kaleidoscope above me.

Lured by the waves and the water and the need for adventure, Fletch and I drove down the coast to spend the weekend on Fripp Island in Beaufort. We went for a Sunday brunch at Palm Fronds, one of the bars overlooking the beach. My fate lay in an ad in the local paper, circled in red, as if God himself had put it there on the table for me to find. "For rent: Garage apartment on the sound. Summer season only. Will consider barter of rent for housekeeping of adjacent rental properties." I could barely manage to eat my French toast for the sweet excitement.

"Fletch, I think this was left here just for us. God knows I need a vacation, a real one, not just a weekend, but for a whole summer. This could change everything. What do you think? Do you think I'll get the job?"

"I think whoever circled that ad on that paper might already have it."

"Don't say that! I'm telling you, this was left here for us. I just know it. Hurry up and finish your pancakes so I can call."

"That's what cell phones are for, Mom. You can call while I eat."

For the first time, I broke my own rule of no cell phones at the table. One call confirmed my belief. The place was available and the owner, Ben, wanted to meet me for an interview later that day. He offered me the job on the spot.

Fletch and I moved to Fripp Island for the summer, the whole summer. Fletch learned to surf and to fish, and after the first week we'd head out together in the mornings. I'd pack him a lunch, cover him in SPF 50, pray to God that he wouldn't drown, get eaten by a shark or kidnapped, and then I'd drop him off at the beach while I cleaned. Within a couple of weeks he had landed a job with our neighbor Drew, a local fishing guide, who paid him in cash.

We'd spend the evenings sitting on the deck, watching the sun set over the sound as we filled our stomachs with fresh fish, oysters, crabs, whatever Fletch had caught that day. We opened the windows to catch the breeze coming off the water and listened to the nightly concert of cicadas and spring peepers. I had just finished the dishes and poured myself a glass of wine and was looking through the bookshelves for a good read when I came across *The Spirit of Honey Hill* by Mabel Jeanine Peppers. I opened the cover and read the inscription.

> *To Joanie-*
>
> *Thank you for all of your help with the Cultural Celebration Day! Our spiritual connection can never be touched, but this is about our land. Lose the land, lose the people. Lose the people, lose the life we have known. We will save Goethe!*
>
> *-Mabel*

As I read each page over the next week, the words sank deep into the heart of me. I read about the importance of rhythm in African culture, the cycles of preparing the earth, planting and then harvesting, and the beating djembe and dunun drums that were used to celebrate the rhythms of life. Rhythm. My world had become stagnant, stuck in the dormancy of winter for far too long, but I could feel something like the early buds of spring beginning to blossom inside, bringing me back to life.

Then for the first time in all my years, I don't know how I had missed seeing it before, but there it was—hope. Like a second sunrise that came at the end of the day, like a new beginning, a second chance, even more beautiful and more brilliant than the real sunrise, mysterious and intriguing. It took me several minutes to recognize it for what it was, the moon rising up over the ocean.

I began to dream again. It was probably the first time in years that I had been rested well enough to remember my dreams. One Sunday afternoon I dreamed that I pulled on my running shoes and headed out the door. I was miles from home and running strong when dark storm clouds began swirling above my head. Something kept telling me to keep to the course, and I'd be safe. Just keep going. There would be shelter at the end of the road. I stayed focused until the lightning came, illuminating the dark sky. It was beautiful, exciting and dangerous all at the same time. Somewhere I lost my focus. I stopped running and stood in the middle of the thunder and lightning, gazing up at this captivatingly beautiful storm, feeling alive for the first time in years. The excitement and the beauty was enough for me to risk the danger. Mesmerized, I stood in the midst of an electrical storm. Like I had been shipwrecked in the Land of the Lotus Eaters, time had passed, and I wasn't sure how long I had been standing still in a stupor, caught between pleasure and peril. Suddenly, I awoke from this fugue within my dream. Fear overtaking me, I knew I had to get out, get back on the road. I ran for the nearest cover, but instead I ended up in the middle of a power station, surrounded by transformers with lightning striking all around me. Just then Fletch climbed into bed with me, waking me up.

"Why doesn't dad just get a real job?"

"I don't know, Hon."

"Doesn't he want to be here with us?"

"Of course he does," I said, even though I often wondered the same thing, and I held him while he cried.

I wanted to finish the dream. My body craved the storm. My mind longed for the beauty of the lightning and the excitement of the thunder. I wanted to know if I made it out safely, but the dream would never come to me again.

I began reading articles about the property tax issues on Goethe. The Colleton family had benefited from the backs of black slaves who had molded the land with their own hands, and once freed, had worked for decades as sharecroppers to earn a piece of property to call their own. Homes built by great-great-grandfathers still stood sheltering the generations.

Every other Gullah community in Beaufort County had been displaced except for Goethe. Unable to keep up with rising property tax increases, descendants in other communities had been forced from acres of waterfront property to slums some twenty miles inland after losing their land at auction. Only a few were able to remain close to the water, but they felt like strangers in the only place they'd ever called home. White people came in building gated communities and called them "plantations." The old ways of fellowship and gathering for feasts after a successful day of fishing were over. The people of Goethe were fighting for their land, for their home, for their culture, for their community.

Goethe was just about a thirty-minute drive and a ferry ride from Fripp. I decided to go see the island for myself and called to arrange a meeting with Mabel Peppers.

"Fletch, I want you to go with me."

"Mom, I can't. Drew's taking these rich people out on their yacht. 'Yacht,' Mom. Did you hear me? Don't make me miss it. We're supposed to be offshore all day. I'll probably get to bring back some fish, and you're the one who read that book anyway. Pleeeeaaase."

"Ok, but I want king crab legs for dinner," I said,

smiling.

"We're not going to Alaska, Mom. Thanks for letting me go. I promise I'll bring back something."

I took the ferry over to the island. I had been told that someone would be waiting at the dock to take me to meet Ms. Mabel, but I didn't know who that someone was. A few minutes later the parking lot was empty, and I was standing there all alone. I waited for a while before I gave up and wandered back down to the dock where a man was fishing.

"Any luck?" I asked. He turned and looked, but didn't say anything. I'd heard people on the island were funny like that. "What you fishin' for?" Still nothing. I sat down. It's not like I had anywhere else to be, and the next ferry wasn't returning to the mainland for eight hours. I was telling him about the book and why I'd come to Goethe when something grabbed his line. I jumped up so excited to see what it was, as he reeled in the biggest fish I'd ever seen anyone catch. I was askin' a million questions all at once when finally he spoke, asking me to put my foot on that fish while he went and got his pliers outta' the truck. "Sure," I said.

He ran to get his pliers. I'd grown up fishing at the lake, mostly brim and a few catfish, so I knew you didn't need pliers to get a hook out 'less the fish just swallows the whole thing. Figuring maybe I could prove myself worthy of a conversation, I reached down to get the hook out myself, and that fish about took my fingers off. Pain shot through my hand. Frightened, I instinctively jerked my hand from its mouth, feeling the skin peel back on my fingers. Frustrated, I pressed my foot hard into its gills and held my hand in a tight fist to ward off the pain. I could see him coming down the ramp to the dock, and I prayed that a giant eagle might swoop out of the sky and kidnap a small dog, or anything that might take the focus off my stupidity.

No such luck. He came back yellin' at me. "Well, you didn't tell me it was a giant piranha! How was I supposed to know? It's not like this is the freakin' Amazon!" He looked like he might laugh which made me even more frustrated. I tried not to cry, pain and embarrassment bringing a red hot heat to my normally tan cheeks. He cut the line, threw the fish back, and packed up to leave. A rush of panic went through my body because my hand really hurt and the ferry was not coming again anytime soon, but I was not about to ask for help. He turned around. Eyeing me, he set down his gear.

"Le' me see." He sighed, his voice starting to soften. He reached out his hand and waited for me to come to him. I looked at him, really looked at him for the first time. His skin was dark and beautiful. There was no doubt that he had been an athlete, probably a football player, which had done him a lifetime of favors leaving him with those beautiful calves and strong thighs. He had hard working hands, his arms muscular, his shoulders and chest broad, and his jawline strong. I finally reached his eyes, and they were firmly settled on mine, patiently waiting. He held my eyes with his for just a moment before he smiled, diverting his glance back to my hand. I didn't like needing him, and I wasn't used to having someone take care of me. I hesitantly held out my arm, and he stepped forward taking my hand in his. He touched me for the first time, and his touch, like his demeanor, was strong but compassionate, and I felt he was someone I wanted to trust.

"You gotta' open your hand so I can see it." Hesitantly I loosened my fist, feeling my pulse rushing through my fingers, trying not to look or flinch. I could feel my heart racing, and I thought I might pass out. He must have noticed because he flipped over his bucket and told me to sit down. Still holding me gently by the wrist, he opened his water bottle and let it wash over my wounds. Promising to take care of me, he took me home and Superglued me back together.

My hand was throbbing. He looked at me, offered me a glass of moonshine, and I knew I was in trouble. My husband was somewhere in South America, and here I was letting another man take care of me, about to open myself up to who knows what. It wasn't like me to be in this situation. It wasn't like me to be in any situation except teaching, grading papers, or cleaning all day. I'm not sure if I ever officially accepted, but there I was, drinking something from a baby food jar, and then another and maybe a couple more. I'm not sure, but it all went straight to my head. I watched him with wonder, listened to his thick Gullah accent pour over me thick and smooth and sweet like molasses. I decided he was the most beautiful man I had ever seen.

He gave me a tour of the island, finally taking me to Ms. Mabel's, the reason I had come to the island in the first place, which I had almost forgotten. I expected him to leave me there, but instead, he wandered over to a live oak, lowerin' himself to the ground, leanin' back against its trunk and closing his eyes as if to take a nap in the shade. I was sittin' at a picnic table, listening to Ms. Mabel tell stories when her grandkids came outta' the little store. They saw Tobias, and they were so excited, runnin' over to him, jumpin' in his lap and climbin' all over him.

He took the kids out in the yard and began showin' them how to throw the football, and I couldn't hear anything Mabel was sayin'. All I could do was watch him coachin' those kids. They were laughin' and havin' so much fun. He was so into them it was like I wasn't even there anymore, and as much as I didn't want to disappear from his sight, I was completely intoxicated. My head was spinnin', but I didn't know if it was the moonshine or him. He went on coachin' the kids like that for an hour or so, 'til Mabel was done. I thanked her and asked her if she had a copy of the book that I could buy and if she would sign it for me.

Then it was time for me to head back to the ferry. He offered to take me, said he was headin' to the dock anyway. He opened the door to the truck for me, and I hopped in. I could feel him studying me, could feel his eyes trace the outline of my body as he shut the door. He walked around the truck, shaking his head, and I couldn't hide my smile. He made me feel beautiful and wanted. It was the happiest that I could remember feeling in years. He had awakened every sense in my being that had been dulled for so long that I had forgotten what it was like to feel. The thought of him made me drunk, and I didn't stop smiling for weeks.

My hand healed, leaving a few tiny scars that I was thankful for. They were the only proof that it hadn't just been a dream. I went to the library to research Goethe, looking for an excuse to return. I remembered the inscription in the book and looked up "Cultural Celebration Day," realizing that the next one wouldn't be for two and a half months. I couldn't wait two and a half months to see him again. I was afraid that he would forget. All I knew was how I felt, and I couldn't shake the thought of him. It seemed like the most real thing that I'd felt in years. Whether he felt it or not, I didn't want to forget what it was like to feel something.

It was the first time I knew for sure that I could leave Levi, the first time that I'd had the energy to seriously consider it. It was the first time I felt convinced that life could be better. It could be more. I realized I was waiting for a man that I had long outgrown to come home, and even if he did come home, it might be too late. I might not be waiting anymore.

Stand on the shores of a site unseen. The substance of this dwells in me 'cause my natural eyes only go skin deep, but the eyes of my heart anchor the sea. Plumbing the depths to the place in between the tangible world and the land of the dreams because everything here ain't quite what it seems. There's more beneath the appearance of things.

- Josh Garrels

5

Jeremiah

I was on security detail at the Courthouse in Dale when I got the call from Sheriff Adams. "Your people got a murder on the island. Barnes is on his way to relieve you, so you can go over and check it out. I've already called the DNR. They're sendin' over the ferry to pick you up."

"Did you really just say, '*my people*,' and what you mean a murder? I know nobody was murdered on Goethe."

"The maintenance boys at the Colleton mansion called it in. Said there was a dead white woman in the bottom of the pool. Said it looks like she got beat pretty bad. I know this'll be your first homicide investigation. You got any questions?"

"Who else is going?" I knew it. I knew he was going to say Nick Jordan. I had been his training officer four years ago when he started, and I had two more years experience than he did, but a case like this was all he needed to push past my glass ceiling, to set sail using my star, and it wouldn't be the first time.

"It's Goethe, Frazier. You and Jordan should be able to cover the whole island in about a half hour, right? We're not wastin' any more manpower on Goethe. This is your people. Y'all just go complete the paperwork and be done with it."

I hated working for Dale. Ain't nothin' of no importance ever happen there. "Wastin' man power?" What the hell did he think was goin' on in Dale? He might interrupt a PTA meeting? If there had in fact been a murder, it was going to affect a lot of people's lives, lives that didn't matter to the Dale Police Department.

I called my father to meet me at the dock with the truck, and double checked the kit to make sure it had everything I needed to process a crime scene.

Of course they sent the *Robert Smalls*, which they shoulda called the Moses 'cause it was slow enough to turn the twenty minute ride into a forty minute cruise.

"Seriously? Have they raised the sails yet? I'm gonna take a nap. Wake me up when we get there." Jordan lay down on a bench of the lower deck.

Leaving him there, I gladly walked to the upper deck and stood outside breathing in the salty air and letting the breeze cool my skin. It had been nearly two years since I'd gone home and ten years since I'd lived there.

Ain't nothin' 'bout Goethe like the rest of the world. It's got its own set a unspoken rules, and 'less you grew up there, you're probably never gonna understand. One time my aunt Pearl came to visit, and she and Mama were fussin' over this and that for three days. After Aunt Pearl went to bed one night, Mama took some hair from her comb and put it inside a little pouch. Early the next morning, before the sun had barely come up, she sent me to creek to catch a fish. "Don't kill it," she said. "You gotta put this hair in the fish's mouth and then let it go."

"Why?" I asked.

"Pearl gonna keep on movin' right outta here, long as that fish keeps swimming." Sure enough, Aunt Pearl had caught the early morning ferry back to the mainland before I'd even made it back home.

A spider buildin' a web in your house meant someone was coming to visit, and that person would be the same color as the spider. It seemed true to me, 'cause we saw spiders all the time, always black or brown, same color as everyone who stopped by.

We had our ways. You don't talk to white people who come on the island. Always make your wishes on the new moon. The oldest folks in the house get the corners of the brownies. Don't go near the water by yourself. Time means nothing. The party starts when people get there, and it ends when they leave.

I never quite fit in with the kids my age on Goethe, my skin lighter, a lil' too light. It takes time for all babies to brown up. Folks looked at my mother and my father and thought for sure I'd darken up eventually, but my skin turned about the color of light brown sugar and then it stopped. High yellow. I didn't look like anybody. Everyone else on the island had the same dark skin as our tribe in Sierra Leone, where our ancestors were from. Their skin, dark as chocolate, was an outward symbol of a rich heritage that was passed down in everything we did, in every tradition, every story that was told to us. We all learned how to weave cast nets on the porches of our grandfathers, and how to cook anything in a hole in the ground from our grandmothers. The healers taught us to make remedies from plants that our ancestors had brought with them on slave ships. There was part of me that was proud to be from Goethe, from Africa, and part of me that carried the burden of buckra skin.

We played the dozens, roasting each other 'til somebody got mad.

"Yo' ankles so ashy, you look like you wearin' socks."

"Yo' so ashy, you look like you been kickin' flour."

"You so ashy, you whiter than Jeremiah," and they would all laugh. That's how I knew it wasn't good to be light skinned on the island.

Other kids could play outside all day and just get darker and darker. I was the only kid on Goethe who'd get sunburned. My folks had to go to the mainland to get sunscreen for me. I used to get burned so bad my skin would bubble up, and I'd run a fever. It'd hurt so bad I couldn't even sleep wid' the sheets touchin' me. My skin would be burnin' like fire, but I'd be shakin', freezin' to death on the inside. Sometimes I thought steam might rise off my skin like when you put a cold, wet log on the fire. All the other kids ran 'round all day smellin' like leaves and dirt, but I was all lathered up in SPF 30, smellin' like a coconut. I was young when I learned what buckra skin was, but older before anyone could explain to me why I had it.

Even though I had the buckra skin, parts of me still looked black. I was too much a combination to fit in anywhere. My mama used to say, "You're a beautiful mystery," but everyone else acted like I was a curse.

"I hate my golden eyes," I'd tell her.

"Those are lion's eyes, straight from Africa," she'd say.

But when I told the other kids that, they'd just laugh. "You might a come from the zoo, but didn't no part a you come from Africa."

My brown hair, soft and curly, was just another reminder of the buckra blood that somehow decided to show up five generations late. Once I was old enough to have a say, I kept it cut as short as possible. My mama wanted me to grow it out, but I refused.

Being on the mainland was a different story. My lips hugged the lips of white girls and wrestled passionately with the lips of black girls. My body put on muscle without me even trying. I could run circles around kids my age in almost any sport. I moved between worlds like no one else could, but at the same time nowhere felt like home. Like an eclipse, I was invisible when I wanted to be seen, and everybody stared at me just when I wanted to disappear.

Content to find my place among white friends at school on the mainland, I was slowly pulled away from my culture. The lightness of my skin separated me on Goethe, and the darkness of my skin drew people to me on the mainland. I was dark enough to qualify as everyone's "black friend," and still light enough to be acceptable. Being chosen was easier than trying to constantly prove myself, even though being the black friend had its limits, and I knew that there were certain things I was too dark for—semi-formal dances and meeting white girls' parents.

Before long kids from the island started calling me

"Tom," some of the older folks too. That's what happens when you appear to be gettin' in tight with white folks from the mainland. People don't trust you so easily, and here I was bringing a white cop from the mainland to interrogate people for the murder of a white woman on our island. It wasn't going to be easy, but like my mama always said, "sugarcane is sweetest at its joint." This was my chance.

My father was waiting as the *Robert Smalls* pulled into the dock. He shook my hand, pulling me close into a hug and whispered, "I'm proud of you, Son." I knew there was another side that was deeply disappointed that I'd left with no intentions of ever living there again. Things had changed so much. When I was a kid we never saw white people on the island, none, and then they started coming over on the ferry, taking tours. My mama would get spittin' mad because they would take pictures of us. It didn't matter what we were doing, tending to the garden, workin' on the truck, ridin' our bikes, or throwin' the football, like they'd never seen a black person before. The first white people since the Colleton family moved to the island when I was a teenager, building a home bigger than four of ours put together. It sat up high on stilts like it was lookin' down on us, and that was their *second* home. That created all kinds of problems for people.

"Dad, this is Nick Jordan."

Nick stuck out his hand, and I smiled as my dad gave him a proper handshake. I tossed my bag in the back of the truck and we headed towards home.

"Take the truck for as long as you need it." The department didn't have any vehicles on Goethe because there weren't any police on the island. "Your mama's been cookin' ever since that woman showed up dead. She knew they'd send you. She misses you, you know."

"Dad, what happened?" My dad was an elder, and I knew the elders would have met and discussed what to do about a dead white woman before ever calling the police. I also knew he probably wouldn't say much with Nick in the truck, but when was Nick not going to be around? That was the whole problem.

"I don't know, Son, but if you really want to find the truth, don't look where she fell. You gotta' find where she slipped."

"Excuse me, Sir. What do you mean 'where she slipped,'?" Nick asked.

Dad laughed. "Never mind," he said.

I knew exactly what he meant. She had brought this on herself. "You think somebody put root on her?" I asked.

"Naw, she's a white woman."

"You mean 'root' as in some African hoodoo voodoo crap?" Nick queried.

"Jesus," I thought, "doesn't he know when to shut up?"

"Don't you have any sense? You can't ask a question like that." Dad laughed. "You don't know Goethe."

Thank God we pulled up to the house, ending the conversation. Mom was waitin' outside with a Tupperware dish full of rice, beans, okra, corn, tomatoes, shrimp, sausage and who knows what else, with a side of sweet cornbread wrapped in foil, a couple paper plates and plastic forks. "Boy, get over here. Don't they have food in Dale?

Lord, you're nothing but skin and bones. I know you gotta get on over to the mansion, but I don't want you goin' hungry. Come back when you done workin', spend the night, talk a while. We're havin' a sweet potato cook-off at the Community Center tonight. Mabel's got chefs comin' all the way from Hilton Head."

She said it like Hilton Head was on the other side of the world. "Alright, Mom. Thanks. I love you." I kissed her on the cheek before headin' out.

"What'd he mean 'Where she slipped'?"

I smiled, shrugging my shoulders. Maybe Adams was right. These were my people. Only a fool has to ask to have a proverb explained to him, and Nick Jordan was definitely a fool. He was here to make a name for himself, and I was here to make sure that it wasn't at someone else's expense. Even though I'd never worked a murder case before, probably no one in Dale had, I knew that evidence could be used to prove whatever Adams wanted, to prove someone guilty who wasn't, and the darker the skin the easier it would be. Once this woman's family started pressuring the department for justice, Adams would find evidence to hold someone accountable, and we were all expendable.

"How the hell did you grow up here with these backwoods crazy ass people? I see why you left."

"Why don't you rest your mouth 'fore it comes unraveled?" Under different circumstances I might've beat the brakes off him, but he didn't even realize the home field advantage that I had, and I'd just as soon let him think we were on the same mission. He clearly thought he was leadin' the way, but without anyone to follow, he was just goin' for a walk.

We stood on opposite sides of the pool, looking down at a dead body completely covered by greedy fiddler crabs feasting on flesh. "Shit!" I jumped down into the pool, crabs scattering everywhere like something out of an *X-Files* episode. "Shoooo! Get!" I yelled as I stamped my feet at a few stragglers.

It was a white woman, badly beaten, just like they'd said. She wore a pair of thin plaid pajama pants and a light grey t-shirt, arms folded across her chest. Her right arm was swollen to a grotesque deformity, splitting at the fingers, bruised in shades of purple so deep her arm looked black against the extreme paleness of her neck and face. Her skin was marked by hundreds of post-mortem wounds inflcted by the tiny pinchers of crabs. Moss cushioned her head against the cement floor. Quarters had been placed on each of her eyelids, flowers by her side, and a small backpack lay beside her.

Nick broke the silence. "Good God, what happened to her? You ever seen anything like this before?"

"Hell no, not on Goethe. Well… not anywhere. This is like out of a movie."

"You know her?"

"Naw, I been gone from the island for almost a decade. I never saw her before. There's plenty of white folks who come to the island. For all we know this was her first time."

Neither of us had ever processed a murder scene. We knew we weren't allowed to touch the body until the coroner had been called, but we both wanted a closer look. I turned to face the same direction as the body. East. Nothing inside of me would ever believe that one of my people had killed her, but I knew this wasn't her first time on the island, and I knew that someone from the island had laid her to rest, someone who cared for her. Burying a body facing East towards Mecca was a Muslim tradition that came from Africa, one of many that we still held in high regard.

Superstitions about the dead were hard to break, and I kept a safe distance. Nick, on the other hand, knelt down by her bare feet, which were light purple. He lifted her pants leg a few inches to reveal purple ankles and legs. He lifted her shirt a few inches, inspecting her pale, ghostly midsection.

Her hand, engorged, splitting, oozing, reached out to me, and my eyes caught a glimpse of something, something white, almost obscured by the fat fingers swollen into a baseball size mitt. A million thoughts went through my mind, feeling the pull of two worlds. Nick gave me no choice. I couldn't trust him.

I sank to the floor of the pool, tucking my head between my knees. "Nick, I… I don't feel so good. I think I'm gonna be sick. Think you could grab me some water from the truck? I'm sorry. I'm just not used to seeing dead bodies."

"Wow, well thank God they sent you to investigate a homicide. Sure, let me get you some water."

Nick climbed the steps out of the pool and headed towards the truck. I scurried towards the dead body, leaning in for a closer look. Sure enough, she grasped what appeared to be a note in her hand. I snatched the folded note card, shoving it into my pocket just as I heard the door to the truck slam shut. Heart racing, body scrambling back to where he'd left me, I resumed my position and waited. I thought of the backpack and wondered what it held, but there was no time left.

"Here. Jesus, you really look like shit."

Face flushed, I struggled to stand, knowing I'd just tampered with evidence, evidence that could potentially convict one of my people for murder. I thought I might throw up at the thought of what I'd just done, at the thought of what might be in my pocket.

"Yeah, thanks. Sorry. I guess I'm just not good with dead people," I said. Half proud of myself and half terrified, I put on my best poker face.

I wondered what he was thinking, but I didn't have to wonder for long. "Lividity. She died in an upright position, and remained that way for some time, maybe twenty or more hours before being laid to rest in this position. You can tell by the way the blood pooled to her lower extremities, staining her skin purple. She hasn't been here, in the bottom of the pool, for long."

"How you know all that?"

"I watch a lot of crime shows. You gotta do your research, Frazier."

"And her arm?"

"I don't know what the hell happened to her arm. That's some crazy looking shit."

We climbed out of the pool and began taping off the crime scene. We searched the surrounding area for trace evidence, footprints, marks where her body might have been drug through the grass, tire tracks, but there was nothing. No cigarettes butts, no gum, nothing. DNR kept the place immaculate.

"Why don't I call the coroner? I'll wait here, keep

the crabs off the body and process it when he arrives. You can get a head start on talking to the DNR boys."

I welcomed the opportunity to talk to people without having to drag Don Johnson along with me. I found the DNR workers taking a break out back near the woods 'bout a hundred yards from the main house. They were all men I knew, some my age. We used to hang together as kids, others old as our fathers. I didn't have to ask their names even though I would have to run background checks on each of them.

"Yo, what's up? Look, it's Tom." They laughed. I gave 'em a nod, taking my seat on an old log. I expected them to rag me pretty hard, but the seriousness of the situation weighed heavily on all of us. We shared a smoke, and I began doing my job, asking questions of people who would be hesitant to say anything. It was hard for me to make small talk. It always had been. Their trust went as deep as the pigment of my skin, and although Goethe had no need for the police, the people aren't ignorant of the struggles on the mainland. It's part of why they work so hard to keep the land. It is its own place, free from a lot of outside authority. My uniform only made things worse. The only thing I knew to do was to be direct.

"I know that none of the descendants killed this woman. I know that, but there is a dead *white* woman lying in the bottom of the pool facing east. I know she knew someone on this island. Someone put that woman in that pool, and only a man would be strong enough to carry that body without having to drag it. I'm not saying that person killed her, but somebody knows something. Y'all gotta' help me out here. Just tell me who she is."

Silence. I waited, lit a second cigarette.

"Look, I'm not asking you who killed her. I *know* it wasn't one of us. I'm just asking who she was. What was her connection to the island? Who did she know here?"

Tortured minutes could be measured in cigarette butts. Finally, Paul answered, "Elanda." Everyone cut their eyes at Paul, insuring that was the first and last word any of them spoke to me. At least it was something. I knew the answers to all of my other questions without having to ask. They arrived at work at eight o'clock a.m. No one had seen anything. They came back from lunch to discover the dead woman in the pool and they called the authorities. Of course they would leave out any mention of the elders meeting to discuss how to handle the situation.

I took the truck and headed to Elanda's place. About halfway there I pulled down a dirt road, far enough that I didn't have to worry about anyone passing by or seeing me reading a note or even holding a piece of paper. I had serious reservations about what I'd done, but I'd done it, and I sure as hell wasn't putting it back now. Parking the truck, I pulled the note from my pocket.

> *You-*
>
> *Happy birthday, my Love. I used to think we could just go our separate ways, make the most of where we are, and I tried, but I can't do it. I don't want to spend the rest of my life without you. I don't want you to do anything different because I know it will hurt your heart. Now's not the time. I never meant for any of this to happen. I didn't know how you would affect me, and now I don't want to*

give you up. You used to say that you wanted all your time with me, and I know I'm on borrowed time. You say you might not be there when the time is right, but I just want you to know that I'm coming for you, and when I do you won't have a choice. No matter what happens, it will never change how I feel about you. Bury this note where you can read it when things get tough, a reminder that we will be together forever one day. Never doubt. One day I am coming for you. Be strong. I love you.

- Me

Everything about it felt wrong, like I'd done more than broken the law, like I'd intruded into their souls, their deepest desires, uncovered some secret. Part of me wondered what he meant when he said, "you won't have a choice." What if he'd come for her, and she didn't want to go so he killed her? What if he *had* killed her, and I, the cop sent to investigate the murder, a descendant, had hidden the most critical piece of evidence? My heart was pounding in my ears and I felt sick, almost maddened that I'd allowed myself to become part of a possible cover up, but there was no going back now. I searched the truck until I found matches in the glove compartment. I stepped outside into the sun, striking the match, holding it just below the notecard until it caught. I held onto this piece of someone's soul as long as I could until I felt the heat burning my fingers. I dropped it to the ground, stomping out the smoldering ends to ensure that the grass wouldn't catch fire. Then I used the heel of my boot to dig a little hole and bury the remnants and the ashes. No one would ever know. I got back in the truck and headed to Elanda's house.

She opened the door like she'd been expectin' me, hugged me and welcomed me inside. A young girl about six or seven years old came running into the room and wrapped her arms around my waist. Instinctively I picked her up.

"What's your name?"

"Jasmine, but most people call me Jazz. What's yours?"

"I'm Jeremiah."

"You here 'cause a the dead woman?"

"Jazzy!" Elanda shouted. She immediately squirmed out of my arms and down my body and ran off to the back of the house.

"That was Jasmine, my granddaughter. Can I get you something to eat or drink?"

"No, Ma'am. I'm good. How are you? How's Jed?"

"Everything is everything," she smiled.

Time is a completely different construct on Goethe. I didn't understand that until I moved to the mainland. Relationships are the most important thing on the island. People work for money, just what little they need. Money is freedom, and freedom is time. Work is something you do to survive. You work the land, you fish, and you do it along side each other. On the mainland, people work for things. Time is money and money is more stuff.

When payday comes, trying to hold onto that check is like trying to hold water in their hands. There's an old Bible verse, "The rich rule over the poor, and the borrower is slave to the lender." Forgetting about the past, people become complacent, exchanging their lives for things, living beyond their means, all the while padding the pockets of opportunistic oppressors who run the usuries.

When you live on Goethe you can't forget 'cause it's all around you. A ditch eight feet wide and five feet deep runs alongside the dirt roads, all over the island. You think about your ancestors digging those ditches under the watchful eye of an overseer. You see scars on the whipping trees, scars that have risen above your head, a measurement of time passed. You think about how hard your ancestors worked just so you could own that piece of the land that had been nourished by their blood, sweat and tears. You're connected. It's all around you.

Twice a year the men and women from the island gather at the beach on a Saturday morning to drag the hundred-yard seine net. One drag of the net will produce enough fish, sharks, crabs and sting rays to feed the entire island for a couple of days. It's a right of passage. I begged my dad to take me when I was about five. "No," he said.

When I wouldn't stop asking "but why?" he told me to go ask Isaiah. Isaiah sat me down, like he had dozens of kids before me, pulling up his pants leg up to his knee.

"You see that scar?" I nodded my head. He took my hand, gently running my soft fingers over the rough cord.

"What happened?"

"When I was 'bout your same age I wanted to go see them drag the seine net. My grandmother said 'no', but I begged and begged and begged 'til my grandfather gave in. When we got there he said, 'You sit right here on the beach and don't move 'til I tell you to. You understand?' And I did just that. I sat right there in that spot. They drug the net up on the shore, and the ground was hoppin' with life. Big ol' fish floppin' all over the place, crabs runnin' this way and that way, even a couple sharks, and I forgot all 'bout my promise. Sure to goodness, I tell you the truth. I didn't mean to move. I just forgot. The men were busy loadin' up the catch and haulin' it to the trucks waitin' on the other side of the dunes, and I got it in me to keep them crabs from runnin' off. I start runnin' all over the place, havin' a good ol' time, 'til I step on a stingray, and its barb shot straight up my leg."

"What'd you do?"

"Lord, I hollered and wailed. What you think I did?" he laughed. "Someone had to get a boat to take me over to the mainland, then drive to the hospital where I had surgery." Isaiah pulled out a jar.

"Open your hand." He poured the contents into my palm. I held the broken pieces of the barb in my hand and looked at that scar, and I decided I could wait.

"When you turn ten, then you can sit on the beach and watch. That's when you're old enough to remember."

"I don't think I wanna go."

"You'll wanna go. 'Cause someday, when you're tall enough to stand alongside the grown folks you'll be the one draggin' the net."

Watchin' them drag the net for the first time was a right of passage. I sat on the shore and listened to my grandfather tell me the story of the Ibo Africans.

"You can feel it. It's the same water that connects you to St. Simon's Island, the site of Ibo's Landing. The Ibo Africans had arrived on slave ships. Ordered off by their kidnappers, they stood on the shore, shackled together at their ankles while white men argued in a foreign tongue. One of the men, a brave warrior called Oba, whispered a plan. At once the Ibo Africans, men, women and children turned back to the water. Bound together, they rushed into the ocean with faith that the water would carry them back home. Death set them free. They became a symbol of fearless defiance. "

At fifteen I stood among men and women, proudly looking back at a few younger kids on the shore watching with eager eyes. Together we waded into the ocean, one group, one huddled mass. Nervous, everything inside of me wanted to be safely on the shore, but we are bound together by more than shackles. We all think of the Ibo Africans, feeling our bodies wrapped in the coolness of the same murky, green water that carried them home.

I think about how hard my ancestors worked so that I could own a piece of land, and as much as some things have changed, I still see my people landscaping the immaculately kept grounds of the mansion while their own houses are falling apart and they struggle to pay the property tax on land that has long been paid for, land that tells the stories that we live by, land that lives and breathes our history.

Our family members are buried alongside their ancestors in Canaan Cemetery. It's a sacred place where we ask permission of our ancestors before entering. A fresh rain uncovers pieces of old dishes and bits of glass from years of families "breaking the chain," to protect the living after a loved one died and to remind us that we would feast together in heaven someday. Tourists walk into that same cemetery like they own it, pocketing pieces of broken plates for souvenirs, stealing pieces of our past.

My mama says, "There's no forgetting about the past on Goethe, and the remembering keeps you alert so that you never let anyone take advantage of you again." Living on the mainland for ten years could never erase the lessons that have been ingrained in me, but it did instill a sense of efficiency that was expected on the job and with other people, and right now it sounded and felt like the tick, tick, ticking of a clock tied to a bomb inside my head as I tried to balance the old and the new, knowing that time would run out, but I wasn't gonna get anywhere fast on the island.

"Elanda, you gotta believe me when I say I know that none of the descendants did this. I am here to protect us. You have to trust me. You know that someone will go down for this. Sooner or later they'll find enough evidence, real or made up, to indict someone. I'm here to make sure that it's the right person, but time will run out soon. I know I just got here, but this thing will hit the news by tomorrow, her family will demand to know something, and I'll start to lose ground. You have to help me stay ahead of this. What happened? I know you know who she is." Elanda sat down at the kitchen table motioning for me to sit in front of her.

"Her name is Maya. She's a Soul Sister. She's been comin' around for about seven years. She just kind of showed up on the island. She volunteered to help with the Cultural Celebration Day every year. Then she started showing up at The Cottages. They found her dead this morning. That's all I know."

"How'd you know her?"

"I'm a sister. We all know each other. She was a writer, and she was working on a book, a love story set on Goethe. She spent a lot of time talking and asking questions, gettin' to know people. Sometimes she came here just to get away."

"What's her last name? "

"Indigo."

"Indigo? Hmm… How is somebody with the last name *Indigo* gonna end up dead like that?" People on the island often painted their doorframes and window frames indigo blue to ward off evil spirits. "Where's she from?"

"Alljoy, south of the Broad River."

"Is she married?"

"She left her husband years ago."

"Why'd she leave?"

"She fell in love with another man, decided to test the depths of the river with both feet."

"And?"

"I think they both got swept away."

"Yeah, well did *he* end up dead in the bottom of a pool?"

"He didn't do this to her."

Ever since I'd read the note I'd been making mental lists of men on the island. Men about her age, men she was likely to fall for, and the list became shorter and shorter. "Tobias?"

She didn't answer, but she didn't have to. Like dozens of other women, Maya must have gotten lost in his charm. Tobias had always been that way, the one to get any woman he wanted, but being a player didn't mean that he was a murderer, too.

"What about his wife?"

"They separated a while back."

"Any chance she did this?"

"No. For a couple years they did their own thing. She left Tobias and Goethe to pursue a singing career in Charleston. Tobias wasn't the only man in her life, and she wasn't the only woman in his. That's just the way it was."

"Did she know Maya?"

"No, and it wouldn't have mattered because if it hadn't been Maya it would've been somebody else, and she knew that when she left."

"Who else did Maya know here? Who'd she talk to?"

"Me, Mabel, Ruth, Elizabeth, Tamar, Esther, Mary, all the Goethe Soul Sisters."

Out of the group Mabel would know the most. Mabel was a collector of stories, and she owned The Cottages where Maya stayed. I found her at the Community Center arranging centerpieces of driftwood and sand dollars, decorations for the cook off.

"Hey, Mabel."

"Jeremiah, it's always good to see you, baby. How you been?" Mabel was like everyone's grandmother. She hugged me, not letting go easily.

"I'm good. You?"

"Woke up to another day, so I'm not complainin'. Listen, I know why you're here. Let's talk at The Sandbar. Now grab some driftwood and sand dollars and help me finish up these tables."

I smiled. It was nice to be treated like family, more

than I'd expected. We took the truck over to The Sandbar where Mabel poured herself a drink.

"I heard she'd been staying at The Cottages." I followed Mabel to the porch where she sat in a rocker. "How in the world did this white woman get in so tight with folks on Goethe? I know how folks are. People on this island aren't gonna talk to just anybody, and y'all lettin' her write a book?"

She laughed. "You know it wasn't like that. People tolerated her, and she just kept comin' around. Jasmine latched on to her. You can imagine how Jed felt 'bout that. Hell, you just couldn't get rid of her. She'd call the GIPS's office fifty times to book a cottage, show up on the ferry and next thing you know she'd have hitched a ride here. You know how I feel about that."

"Why'd she come here this weekend?"

"She finished her manuscript, wanted me to read it, said she wanted my blessing."

"What'd you say?"

"I told her she should write about white folks."

I laughed. "You have it?"

She handed me a three-ring binder filled with pages, Maya's story. Slipped inside the clear plastic cover was the picture of an attractive young woman sitting on a beach, staring out at the ocean, the image framed by a whimsical looking tree covered in cherry blossoms. "*Sway of the Siren.*" I opened the binder and read the first page, a blurb that I suppose would have appeared on the back cover of the book someday.

> *Sway of the Siren is a brilliantly crafted story of redeeming love and relentless pursuit of a*

woman's heart. Set in the Lowcountry, Goethe Island is one of the few remaining untouched Gullah/ Geechee cultures, fighting to retain the physical connection to their land and their heritage. Maya Indigo struggles against her own forms of oppression. Tired of clumsily waltzing her way around the dance floor with an imaginary partner, she finds herself enticed and enveloped by the Sway of the Siren, discovering a new rhythm that mysteriously matches the beat of her own heart, releasing her from her orbit to spin and twirl and laugh and dance, really dance. In the end, it's only the redemption song of her true love that can carry her back home.

"I'm gonna take this copy. I'll read it tonight. It might have to be considered evidence, but I'll get it back to you as soon as I can."

"Take your time."

"I wish I could. What do you think about her ex-husband?"

"He never came to the island. I know it was a rough marriage. She got tired of using her own feathers to build a nest. Years and years of that left her bare. I tried to tell her, 'You gotta take care a da' roots, you wanna heal da' tree,' but she said 'the roots dried up a long time ago. Besides,' she said, 'There's a whole forest out there, and I'm gonna find me a good oak tree, somebody strong.'"

"You think he had anything to do with this?"

"He lives in South America most of the year, and word would have gotten 'round if there'd been a strange white man in Honey Hill."

"What 'bout Tobias?"

"Tobias, her new song. You know Tobias didn't do this. A couple of years ago Maya was staying here, and I had this dream 'bout her. She was holdin' a cat, not just any cat, but a huge grey tabby cat. Fat. All of a sudden the cat started squirmin' and makin' all kinds of noises so she set it down real quick. The cat started hackin' and coughin', and out comes a baby snake, right outta that cat's mouth, alive as it can be, poisonous too, and it slithered away, fast as lightning. I knew then that something bad was gonna happen to her. She was messin' round with somethin' she shouldn't a been, and one day it was gonna be more than she could handle. I told her so. I'll never forget how she stared at me. She just said, 'I know.'"

I knew the snake was just a symbol of something that gripped her heart and seduced her soul, something she couldn't free herself from. "You think that's what killed her?"

Mabel nodded, pouring herself another drink. I could tell she didn't want to talk about it anymore. Dreams carry a lot of weight on Goethe, and Mabel had the sight, a blessing and a curse. Her dreams often told who was going to get married, who would have a baby, who was going to prosper and sometimes who was going to die, and right now the weight of that gift felt heavy.

There was a loss. I'd never met Maya Indigo, but I sensed it too, knowing I've felt that same pull, enticed and enveloped by it. That could be any one of us at the bottom of that pool. So deft in its deception, temptation sells you the lie that sin appears the most beautiful promise on the brink of paradise, possessing the possibility of satisfying your soul, and you need grace just to *see* evil for evil.

God can restrain the madness of a fool. He can bring His truth through the mouth of a mule. You can move a mountain without any tools. It just takes the faith of a little seed to make a way through what might seem to be an impossibility, and the ability will match the occasion. The outcome will defy explanation. The liberation will not be televised when it arrives like lightning in the skies.

- Josh Garrels

6

Nick

I sat on the side of the pool, shooing away fiddler crabs, my feet hanging over the edge as I stared at the dead body of a badly beaten white woman. I tucked some Copenhagen in my bottom lip and felt my body relax. Sheriff Adams had called me and Jeremiah to investigate the scene of the crime. I was looking to make sergeant in the next year, and Jeremiah, well, these were his people. I'd worked hard to get where I am, keeping my nose clean for four years, no internal affairs' investigations. There had been that one excessive force complaint, but thankfully it was dropped.

Jeremiah was my training officer back when I started four years ago. I'm sure he'd probably like to make sergeant too, but we both know it's a long shot. It's common knowledge that he's already been passed over for a couple of positions. Of course he'll tell you it's 'cause he's black. How many times have I heard that? We all have the same opportunities in this life. Some people take advantage of them and others don't. Hell, Jeremiah couldn't even handle the sight of a dead body. How can someone expect to move up in this kind of job if he can't process a crime scene without losin' his lunch?

He took one good look at that body, and I thought he was gonna pass out. So I offered to stay and wait for the coroner to show up while he went around the island asking questions, trying to figure out who this woman was and what happened to her. After all, the only reason Jeremiah had been assigned to the case was because Sheriff Adams knew people were more likely to talk to him, and he was more likely to understand what the hell they were saying, with all their Africanisms. Besides, it's the body that tells the story. You can't expect a bunch of black people to tell you how they killed a white woman, and obviously she didn't put herself in the bottom of this pool.

I was no stranger to Goethe, even though it was my first time being on the island. Everybody in Beaufort knows about the property tax issues. I guess the descendants think since their ancestors were slaves back in the day they shouldn't have to pay taxes like the rest of us, and then they act shocked when the county takes their land.

Last October I had security detail on the steps of the courthouse as they auctioned off properties to the highest bidder. This old black man stood on the steps, hands raised up in the air, calling out "Please don't bid on this one. This is heirs' property. Please don't bid on it." I've seen that work, but not this time. This one must have been waterfront, 'cause that bid just kept going up and up. Those people thought the taxes were high. Shoot, they're never gonna see that land again at eighty thousand. If they want it back, they've got one year to cough up back taxes, plus a percentage of the selling price, plus taxes for the current year. I almost feel sorry for them.

The man's wife started crying. "White folks don't care about us. They don't care. The county doesn't care." Then it started to get personal. "Do you know what my ancestors went through to get that land? How hard they worked? They paid for that land with their blood and sweat. That property has been in my family for nine generations, nine generations, and you just gonna take it. That land means nothing to you. Nothing." The buyer, a man dressed in golf attire, handed his check to the clerk, got in his convertible BMW and drove away, probably making it to the country club in time for tee-off.

It wasn't just at the courthouse or on the local news either. They'd managed to get *CNN* and *The New York Times* all the way down here on this little island interviewing folks. I bet you they weren't calling *CNN* to report the dead body of a white woman in their swimming pool. Wouldn't reporters have a field day with that?

I couldn't stop staring at her body, her arm, her fingers literally split open. Flies swarmed around her like a piece of road kill as maggots danced under her skin. I wondered if this had been a random act of violence or if she had gotten what was coming to her. It was probably some black man who couldn't afford to bring a Cadillac over to the island, so he got the next best thing, a white woman.

It's all about the choices you make, and the people on Goethe are no different. They wanna live here. They just don't wanna pay to live here. It's their own fault for not paying their taxes or for selling off land in the first place. That's why they're in this situation. Then they gonna complain about not having trash pickup, like they want all the conveniences of the mainland without any of the accountability. Now they got a dead white woman on their hands. This was gonna be interesting.

I heard a truck comin' down the road. It was one of the locals, comin' to drop off Nat Tidwell, the Coroner from Beaufort County. He got out, carrying a big black bag and a stretcher, the kind you see paramedics carrying on rescue shows. He ducked under the crime scene tape. I met him halfway, shaking his hand. We walked to the pool where he set down his gear and peered over the side at the body.

"Wow, now that's not something you see everyday, is it?"

"What, a white woman on Goethe or a dead woman in the bottom of a dry swimming pool?"

"Both," he laughed. "Y'all figure out who she is yet so we can contact the next of kin?"

"Not yet."

"Well, let's get started." He picked up his bag and headed down the steps, and I followed.

"Any idea what happened?"

"No. When we first got here she was covered in fiddler crabs. I got the area taped off and we looked for trace evidence but didn't find any, no tire tracks or drag marks, no footprints, nothing. I sent my partner to start asking questions, and all I've been able to do since then is fight off the army of crabs."

"Alright. The first thing we need to do is photograph the scene. You got your camera?"

"Yeah."

"This your first murder?"

"Yeah." He talked me through the pictures and angles, making sure that we had everything digitally frozen before touching anything. It's a good thing the department finally went digital, a hundred and twenty-eight pictures of nothing but this woman's body with her grotesquely swollen arm and the occasional fiddler crab. I hoped I had managed to capture whatever it was I was supposed to find.

We both gloved up, and then I watched as he carefully removed the quarters from her eyes with tweezers, like a grown man playing *Operation*. He placed them in evidence bags, labeling each one. I collected the flowers and the moss. Then we started with her backpack. He pulled the drawstrings and reached in pulling out a Tupperware container, a water bottle and an iPhone. He unscrewed the water bottle and smelled it. "Moonshine." We dusted each one for prints, labeling and sealing them. Then Nat handed me a paper bag.

"You bag that hand, and I'll get this one." Thank God he took the giant eggplant hand. We both secured the bag, wrapping her wrists with masking tape. He held her arm, inspecting the damage done by the fiddler crabs. "Well, they had a feast, didn't they? There must be hundreds of post-mortem wounds, maybe more. Makes her look like a fucking meth addict, doesn't it?" He looked at her feet, lifting her pants leg, just as I had done.

He stood, stretching his arms and legs like he was about to go for a run. "I'm gonna need your help rolling the body over to check under it. You take the legs, and I'll get her upper body." With one big heave we had her on her side. We both inspected the cement for evidence, but there was none. There were no wounds on her back, nothing. He lifted her shirt just a bit, to reveal a line of demarcation, her lower extremities a deep purple from the settling of her blood that faded into a light lavender as it moved up her back, blending into a deathly shade of gray.

"She was definitely sitting upright when she died, and then someone moved her here," I said.

"That's good. How'd you know that?"

"*First 48.* How long would you say she's been laying in this pool?"

"She was probably sitting up for some twenty hours. I'd say she's only been lying down for a few hours, maybe four or five at the most." Beyond that lividity, there was nothing more, just a ridiculously swollen arm. "Hold her right there while I get the body bag." I moved to the middle, with one hand on her hip and the other on her shoulder to keep her on her side.

Suddenly, a fiddler crab crawled out from the top of her pajama pants and ran up my arm. I dropped the body, jumping around, shaking my arms all over the place, screaming, "Mother fucker!" Dale just looked at me. "What? It was crab… on my arm." I smiled.

He sighed. "Don't act like you never had crabs before. Let's get this body rolled back over so we can bag her, and I can go home." We rolled the body back on its side. Nat unzipped the Tyvex bag, sliding it as far under her as possible. We slowly rolled the body onto her back, tucking her arms and legs inside the bag, then zipped it shut. We stood on either side of her, looking down at the giant cocoon.

"What do you think happened?" I asked.

"Hell if I know. One thing's for sure. She didn't do this to herself. Look where she is, a white woman on Goethe. What do you think happened to her?"

"You ever see anything like this before? I mean, her arm?"

"Never. It's the damndest thing I've ever seen. I mostly deal with car accidents and gun shot wounds, pretty straight forward. Hopefully the autopsy and the toxicology reports will tell us something. Help me get this body outta here." He brought over the stretcher and we rolled the body over onto its side, repeating the process. We squatted down on opposite sides of the stretcher and taking the handles, lifted on the count of three. I thought there was no way the two of us were going to get that body up the steps.

"Jesus, they don't call it 'dead weight' for nothing, huh?"

"You got that right."

I was surprised to see the man who'd dropped Nat off still waiting in his truck. We slid the body in the back and shut the tailgate. We packed up our things, and Nat told me that I'd be riding with him to the dock to help load the body in the boat. The ambulance was already waiting on the mainland to transport the body to the hospital in Beaufort.

We rode in silence, a clear division of race and suspicion separating us from our driver. When we arrived at the dock Nat and I carried the body, placing it on the boat.

"You should hear from us in about six to eight weeks." We shook hands, and I watched until the boat had nearly disappeared into the horizon. I turned, hoping the local was waiting to take me back to the mansion, but no such luck. My bags were waiting in an empty parking lot. I pulled out my phone to call Jeremiah, but there was no service. Why the hell anyone would want to live on this island was beyond me. I waited there for two hours until Jeremiah finally showed up.

"What you been doin', havin' a family reunion?"

Jeremiah laughed. "You mad?"

"Hell, yeah, I'm mad. I'm out there chasing off crabs and baggin' some dead white woman's hands. Then I'm sittin' my ass out here in the hot sun for two hours while you're probably gettin' some and eatin' shrimp and grits."

Jeremiah laughed like it was the funniest thing he'd ever heard.

"Well, what the hell'd you learn? You better a found out somethin' good."

We rode the ferry back across to the mainland. Jeremiah talked like he thought he'd solved the whole crime. Her name was Maya Indigo. She'd been coming to the island for years, and had written a book, something she'd hoped would spotlight the oppression of the people and how they were being run off their little piece of land. I guessed she was some Civil Rights activist born too late. Her husband was huntin' gold in South America or something crazy like that. Otherwise, all he had was just some story 'bout a woman on the island and dreams about snakes and visions. It all just reaffirmed my notion that talkin' to any of these people with their voodoo and crazy African superstitions and beliefs was nothin' more than a complete waste of time.

Feel the wind blow, through the window. I know, that we'll make it through. It's a million miles from, where we begun, and I, I still love you. I remember, as clear as ever, the day, when we first met. Lord, you know I, I love to hold her eyes in mine everyday since.

- Josh Garrels

7

Levi

My muddy life. Glimpses of gold. Emails from Fletch. Missing Maya.

My daydreams interrupted by the sound of my name being called urgently. "Levi! LeeeeeVi!!!!"

Annoyed, I stopped the excavator to see what my dad wanted. It was about the tenth interruption of the morning.

"What now?"

"There's a call for you in the office. It's the police department in Dale, South Carolina, says it's an emergency."

Fletch was my first thought. I scrambled down from the machine and ran to catch the call, praying it wouldn't get dropped. Dale. Dale. Dale. What the hell was in Dale, South Carolina?

"Hello?"

"Is this Levi Indigo?"

"Yes, it is."

"Is Maya Indigo your ex-wife?"

"She is. Is everything ok?"

"This is Detective Adams calling from the Police Department in Dale. I'm so sorry to have to inform you that the body of your former wife was discovered this morning on a little island off the coast, Goethe Island. It appears that she was murdered."

Gripped by a numbing horror, I managed to ask, "Does my son, Fletch, know yet?"

"No, maybe it would be best if you were the one to tell him. Can you catch the next flight back to South Carolina? We need someone to identify her remains, and your son needs to know."

"I'll be there. I'll let you know as soon as I've made arrangements. What happened to her?"

"Sir, I can't tell you anything more. Right now there are a lot of unanswered questions. Anything I could share with you would just be speculation at this point."

My heart broke. My legs buckled, and I fell to my knees. I thought that by coming back to Guyana it would give her space to find the truth that I knew was in her soul. Whatever it was, it was the opposite of truth that would leave her dead in some pool.

I threw a handful of things into a backpack, and Dad drove me to the airport. Murdered. My wife, ex-wife murdered. Escaping any hope of sleep, my mind raced as I imagined her being gone forever, but it still didn't seem real. Our marriage had been tough. Impossible. Maybe I should've fought harder to hold on to her. Maybe I should've stuck around. Maybe she'd still be alive.

It had been six years since our divorce. I came home from Guyana expecting nothing. There had been a time when she would tackle me in the airport, and we'd end up finding some back road where we could pull off and make love before we even got home. Sometimes friends and family would be waiting like a real welcome home party, and at the very least she would get dressed up and cook a nice dinner. But things have a way of changing. I'd learned over the years not to expect anything more than for Maya to pass by me on her way out the door to hang with friends, a night out, a break. That's all I was to her, and I resented her for it.

I arrived at the airport only to take a taxi home. She had quit picking me up years before. Fletch was spending the night with a friend, and she had already gone out for the evening. I let myself in to an empty house. Alone. There on the counter was an envelope with my name on it. Divorce papers.

The pipeline cracked. The world exploded around me. A leak turned to an uncontrollable flood of black filth tainting everything it touched. My anger like oil, dark as night, blocked out any light. I had never known grief like that.

She had no idea the things I put myself through, or the risks that I took on a daily basis, trying to provide a future for our family. She had no idea the stress that I felt knowing she was back home carrying the burden for my failures, the desire that I had to succeed, to show her that I'd been worth the wait, but the last thing I expected was for her to leave. Love was a choice and marriage was a commitment for life. We didn't believe in divorce. We believed in longsuffering.

She came home, half drunk, wearing a strapless dress that barely covered her ass. I wanted to talk, but she was passed out before we could have any kind of real conversation. I watched her for hours, sprawled across our bed, snoring, drooling. She was more beautiful than when we'd first met fifteen years ago. Her feet were rough, dry, cracked, like she'd been going barefoot all summer. Her legs were more tan and more fit than the last time I'd seen her. I imagined every inch of her underneath that dress, her curves, the scar on her left hip. She was wearing glasses. When the hell did she get glasses? Taking them off her face and setting them on the side table, I covered her with a blanket and lay down beside her. I wondered if she had been unfaithful and the thought was enough to drive me insane. Losing her was not an option. I didn't care what she had done.

How had I managed to mess this up so badly? My mind went in circles as I began thinking about things from her point of view. She had begged me to stay for years, but I kept going back. It was easy to tell myself, and everyone else that I was doing it for my family, but the truth is there was a lot of freedom to be found living in South America. I had convinced myself that I hadn't failed as long as I refused to give up. There was always hope in the jungle.

I had all night to sit and watch her and think about the last fifteen years. I had not been there to listen to her concerns, fears, successes, failures, loves, hates, wants, dreams or needs. I had not been there to make her feel beautiful, loved or desired. I had not given her my undivided attention. I had taken her for granted, taken advantage of her work ethic, used her, and she was no kind of victim. She never had been. I had always just thought of her as such a strong woman. That was why we worked so well together. I wasn't able to offer her security, but I didn't think she was the kind of woman to need those things from a man.

I had chosen my work and family in Guyana over her for years. I had chosen my own way. She had called me out on it again and again, but I had refused to listen. For years she used to cry every time I'd get ready to go back.

"You're killing parts of me. I'm tired of living life by myself, tired of carrying the burden for everything," she'd yell.

I'd yell back, "You've never supported me."

"Never supported you? Who do you think pays all the bills? Who do you think raises our son so you can do what you do? How is that not supporting you? That's all I've ever done is support you!"

Words wore us thin, and like a match to a leaky fuel line, emotions exploded. After a while she quit crying when I'd leave, and she quit yelling when I was home. I thought it was because she had come to accept things, but now I looked at her and wondered who she had become. She was different.

She woke up the next morning, fixed her coffee and headed out without two words, and I realized exactly how far apart we had grown. I wanted to follow her, wanted to make things right, but I didn't know where she'd go. I didn't know who to call because we were living two separate lives. Chasing her would be the same as her trying to find me in the jungle of Guyana. Her world was completely foreign to me. I would make her understand. I would have to convince her to move to Guyana. No more traveling. We would just move there. She could homeschool Fletch.

I lay there for thirty more minutes before I made my coffee and checked the file cabinet for their passports. They were still good for two more years. I was on the phone booking three plane tickets to Guyana when she walked back in from what I guessed was her morning run.

"Why *three* tickets?"

"I'm taking y'all back with me." When I said the words I realized how stupid that must've sounded to her.

"No, you're not."

"I want you to see what I do, what I've been doing, for us, for our family."

"You wanna see what's been done for our family? Take a look around! You haven't done shit for our family, and we're not going anywhere with you."

"I'm not going to lose you."

"You lost me years ago," and with that she grabbed a towel and headed for the shower, locking the door behind her.

I waited. Thirty minutes later she passed by me with her keys in her hand and started to walk out. I caught her by the arm.

"We have to talk."

"There's nothing to say. What did you expect?" She jerked her arm away. I wanted to grab her, shake her, keep her from leaving, but I knew I didn't deserve that. I didn't have the right to demand to know anything. She was right.

From her point of view I had pretty much abandoned our marriage and left her to make a life for herself, and that's exactly what she had done.

"Please, just tell me where you're going."

"I have a meeting."

"With a lawyer?"

"No, I've already done that. Didn't you get the papers? I'm meeting with an artist. He's been designing a tattoo for me. You know, the one you always said you'd do, but never made time for?" and with that she walked out. I followed her out, watching her back her car down the driveway.

Fit and tan. New glasses. Tattoo. Divorce papers. I wasn't stupid. I thought about private investigators, a tracking device for her car, lawyers, child custody, settlements. My mind fast forwarded about two years, and then stopped abruptly. What I wanted was her heart, something I feared I'd never truly had. She was like trying to hold on to a flame, holding on too tightly would suffocate her and too loosely would leave her to die in her own wildfire.

Going back inside, I pulled out my sketchpad and started drawing. She had talked about it for years. I knew exactly what she wanted, and I knew that unless she came home with it already tattooed on her body that I could design it better than anyone. Even though we'd grown apart, I still knew her curves. Her skin. I knew her style.

I began with the rock, the one thing she'd never mentioned, but I had imagined the drawing for years, and I knew that it began with the rock that would anchor the tree to the lower right side of her back. The rock was God. The foundation. There would be waves, pulling at the roots, tempting them like sirens, but the roots would cling to the rock, and out of it would grow a beautiful cherry blossom tree, fitting her curves just so and blossoming out across her back and over the top of her shoulder. She had always said that the tree should be dead. "Dormant," I'd remind her, but I decided that it needed to be living. As I drew each flower, each petal, each leaf, I prayed that it wasn't too late. I turned on the computer and started researching cranes until I found the one I liked, one with its wings spread so that it looked as though it were about to take flight. The bird would go right in the middle, extending from her side all the way to the center of her back. In the bird's beak was an egg, a symbol of the future. Finally I filled in a couple of clouds and petals raining down from the tree. I turned on the computer and scanned in the drawing to begin smoothing out the lines and adding color. I fell asleep at the desk, and it wasn't until the next morning that I realized she never came home. Fletch was up playing X-Box when I heard the door open. I stood in the kitchen with my coffee. I wanted to be mad, I wanted to know where she had been, and more importantly, who she had been with, but I knew better.

"So how did your meeting go?"

"What meeting?"

"With the tattoo artist?"

"Oh, yeah. He lost the drawing, said someone must've thrown it away when they were cleaning up the shop. So he said he'd try to sketch something this week and he'd give me a call when it's done." She poured her coffee, avoiding eye contact with me.

"I have something to show you."

"If it's a plane ticket, you can keep it."

I went to the office and brought back the drawing, laying it out on the counter. She didn't say anything. I just watched her. I watched her fingers trace the lines of the rock and tree, the blooms. She reminded me of when I was a kid and this stray cat had a whole litter of kittens under our house, and we spent the whole summer trying to tame them and lure them out. I stood motionless, fearful that one wrong move might scare her off. She stood over it for the longest time, and finally, a smile. I breathed. She looked at me for the first time since I'd come home.

"It's amazing. I don't know what to say. It's more beautiful than I would've ever imagined. It's blooming, and that's perfect because I've never felt more alive."

She looked at me, knowing those words stung, but I held my tongue, refusing the urge to come back at her. She waited for my response, and when it didn't come she softened a bit going back to the drawing.

"The rock. It's my favorite part. I can't believe you drew this. How did you know?"

"I know you better than you think." I smiled. "I can sketch it on you if you wanna see what it will look like, see how it fits your body."

She thought about it for a minute. "You don't have to do this. It's not going to change anything. You're an amazing artist, and this is your work. You don't owe me anything, and I don't owe you anything. If you don't want me to have it, it's ok."

"I know. I wasn't trying to... I just wanted to do this for you if it wasn't too late." I followed her to the bedroom where she slipped off her T-shirt and bra. She lay down on the bed. I set the paper next to her and pulled up a chair.

I began with the rock. Taking my time, I knew how rare it was for her to be vulnerable, for her to let me do something for her. It might be the last time. Neither of us spoke. I was content to share the air and be close. Thinking about all of the times she had been my canvas, when I had painted her body before making love to her, how we learned that blue paint stained her skin, gaining unwanted questions. Our secrets. It was the most intimate we had been in years, and there were moments I had to walk away just to keep from losing it. Where had the years gone, and why had I stayed away for so long? She lay perfectly still for almost an hour while I worked.

"You're gonna have to sit up for me to finish the flowers on the front of your shoulder." She stood facing me. In that moment, even without words, I could see her soul as bare as her chest, and I felt the heaviness of her heart. I took my time. "Maybe I should add color."

"No, it's okay. You've done enough." She stood and walked to the bathroom, looking over her shoulder in the mirror. She was a mix of emotion, smiling through tears like sunshine in the rain. "Thank you. It's so beautiful," and she wrapped her arms around me, pressing her body against mine. "Are you sure you want me to have it? This doesn't mean that things are going to turn out the way you want them to."

"I'm sure, Maya. You remember that verse you used to always say, that one about waiting making the heart sick, but a dream fulfilled is like a tree of life? I get it. I really get it. I know this is going to take a lot of work, but I'm willing to work on it, and I'll never leave you again. Just please, don't give up. Don't quit. Not yet."

She grabbed her shirt, slipping it over her head.

"First of all, you quit years ago. Second, I'm done working on it. That's all I've ever done is work, and I know it might be selfish, but I just want to have some fun for once. I'm done. A real estate agent is coming by with some papers for you to sign. I'm putting the house on the market. I found a teaching job at the beach, and Fletch and I are moving."

There actually was an oil spill in the Gulf that summer, the worst oil spill in US history. Two hundred million gallons of oil defiantly and violently erupted through any attempt to plug it, tainting the beautiful ocean, ruining people's vacations. It absolutely couldn't be stopped. My grief turned to anger, and the news reports about the oil spill might as well have been about my heart. I was mad at God because I had faith he would take care of us. I had spent the last thirteen years trying to provide for my family only to lose it all, and I was mad at myself for having naively stayed in Guyana for so long.

It was almost too much to handle. Just like the scientists, I had to figure out a solution, how to handle the spill of my life. I had tried for years plugging the gaping hole with "wisdom," scripture and prayer, but when it didn't hold, the same story got old, and now my wife was saying to me, "Forget this filth. Forget this mess. I'll just get a hybrid and then I'll need you less," forgetting the rich resource I used to be, and switching the channel like I was yesterday's depressing news.

The house sold in three weeks, and she and Fletch were gone. Solitude set in as another family moved into the only home I'd ever known with her. Our marriage was over just as I was learning what it meant to love her for the first time. She had given me half of the equity from our house, a payoff for her conscience, but still more than I deserved, more than my father had ever given me in a share of gold, enough to start a new life for myself. I could go anywhere and do anything, but for the first time, my greatest desire was to be with Maya and to love her well. I owed her that.

It was like she wore a sign around her neck. "Caution- Life under construction. Don't dive in if you can't swim, because I'm the one who needs rescue." Determined to be her savior, I dove in. There were times that the fight in her drug me to the bottom, threatening to create two casualties. I'd retreat to catch my breath and then dive right back in again and again.

Freedom and hope and joy filled the space of oppression as I gave up the title of sharecropper in the jungle of Guyana. I found myself undone by being done, changed by my refusal to change, freed from fear by my own failure. Losing my wife was a sobering reality. So I moved to the beach, got an apartment, a suit, and a surfboard. I landed a job doing construction on Hilton Head with the agreement that I would start in one month.

Pursuit.

Years ago Maya had seen a documentary about a luxury tree house community, a treetop Ewok village hidden in the rainforest of Costa Rica, *Finca Bellavista*. She had called to tell me all about her dream of living there someday. Of course I'd only half listened, telling her I could build a tree house for her in Guyana if she wanted to live in the jungle, which just turned into another fight about my family.

That was the only dream I could ever remember her sharing with me. I called and booked two round trip flights to Costa Rica and reserved the largest, most luxurious tree house in the village. Now I just had to convince her to go. Standing in the floral department of Publix, it hit me that I had never bought flowers for her before. I showed up on my ex-wife's doorstep, with a combination of roses, wild flowers, carnations, and a pot of mums because I had no idea what she liked, and two plane tickets to Costa Rica.

"Seriously, are you insane?"

"Maybe. You said you just wanted to have fun."

"Shit. What's the matter with you?" I could see her trying to hide her smile. "So did you make separate sleeping arrangements for us? 'Cause I'm not having sex with you."

"I'll take a sleeping bag."

"I'm just kidding. Well, about the arrangements part. Ok, I'll go, but we are not getting back together. I'm only in it for the tree house and the tan." She smiled.

Our first night we stayed in a condo at the top of a hill with a balcony overlooking the ocean. I carried our bags in and gave her some space to get ready for dinner.

"You see that restaurant right there? I'm gonna go ahead down there. Come when you're ready." An hour later she walked in wearing a pair of old faded blue jeans and a black strapless top that showed off her tattoo, the one I'd designed. She'd gotten it.

"Wow! Turn around." She spun around, smiling, biting her lower lip, as she always did when she was nervous.

"Well, what do you think?"

"Whoever designed that for you is a hell of an artist. I mean, it's like he knew your body and your heart. I can't believe it. It's amazing. Seriously though, it makes me really proud to see it on you." Just then the server came with two fresh blueberry margaritas garnished with star fruit.

"Thank you. I'm proud to wear it."

"That's a good thing, 'cause it's on there forever now, huh?" I lifted my glass, "Forever."

We spent the next two weeks traveling the coast, surfing, exploring beaches, waterfalls and jungles. We stayed in the Ewok village, our own little world. Our tree house was better than any dream. It was divided into two parts connected by a suspension bridge some eighty feet off the ground. On one end, a beautiful kitchen and luxury stone shower, with a four foot by four foot open window into the jungle. On the other end of the bridge was a sitting area with a spiral staircase leading to another bathroom and the bedroom. Everywhere we looked there were live cut orchids, on pillowcases, on countertops and window openings, tucked into the fold of the washcloths and towels.

The first thing Maya did was insist on running across the suspension bridge in nothing but her rain boots. I was beginning to understand what she meant when she proclaimed she'd "never felt more alive." It was true. There was a spark in her that I'd never known before.

After a full day of hiking and swimming in the river, we returned to our tree house to shower and get ready for dinner.

"You can go first," I said.

"Don't be stupid. Dinner starts in less than an hour and we still have to hike down to the dining hall. Just come on," she said, grabbing me and pulling me into the shower with her.

Steam rose out of the box and through the open window. I took a deep breath, telling myself not to expect anything, and then she started kissing me, pushing me against the cold hard wall, her body pressed against mine. I had never wanted her more in my whole life.

"Oh my God, I can't do this." I couldn't believe I just said that.

"Why not?"

"The wall's too cold, and the bench is too," I laughed.

"Well, come on!" She rinsed off, grabbed a towel and her rain boots, and ran across the suspension bridge to the bedroom. I chased her across the bridge and up the spiral staircase. I don't know if it was being in the jungle, the canopied bed and pillows adorned with live orchids or knowing that she wasn't mine, but it was exotic and erotic. She was free. She did things I'd never known her to do before, but it was only her mind and her body that were free. Her heart was guarded, and it was her heart I was after this time.

After, I lay in the bed and just watched her. She slipped on a sundress and boots.

"Come on. Let's go. It's time for drinks and dinner."

"Why wasn't it always like this?"

"Because you weren't there."

"It could *be* like this."

"It *could've* been like this. I'll see you at dinner," and she walked out.

I spent the next five years in pursuit of her heart, but all she would give me was her body, and sometimes in the middle of it all I could tell myself, "This is all I need. Hell, it's more than most people have," but I was always left wanting more.

Our relationship was like Newton's Third Law of Motion: For every action, there's an equal and opposite reaction. The more I tried to push my way into her life, the more she pushed back.

I learned about her world, and I showed up in every way for every event. For her birthday Fletch helped me steal the key to her classroom. I picked him up like we were going to the movies. Instead, we jumped the rusty barbed wire fence that surrounded her school, breaking into the old portable and decorating the whole room. I covered her dry erase board with Post-It notes to spell out "I LOVE YOU," with a giant pink heart. On the back of each Post-It note I wrote a word to describe her. Then I covered her desk with bright orange roses and pieces of dark chocolate. I bought extra flower petals that I scattered, forming a path from the door to her desk.

"You really think y'all will get back together?"

I laughed. "I don't know, but I figure I don't have anything to lose."

"How about your pride?"

"My pride is the reason I lost her to begin with." Maybe Fletch could learn from my mistakes.

Valentine's Day was approaching, and I knew I better make it good. She'd never been a fan. I used to think every woman loved Valentine's Day, but not Maya.

She used to say, "I don't want flowers and cards and candy on that one day so you can check it off your calendar. I want a man who's willing to show up and love me on all the other days of the year."

"Maya, I live in another country."

"I know. That's the problem."

Every year she was invited by Delta Sigma Theta, the largest African American sorority, to attend their Valentine's Day Gala. She'd go with her girlfriends to drink and dance the night away. She asked me to take her every year, but I never went, even if I was home. Dancing was pretty much my greatest nightmare, and a gala was the last place on earth I would ever want to be under any conditions. The next thing I know I'm begging her best friend to sell me a ticket to this year's gala.

"Is she going with someone else? Because if so, I understand."

"She's going with friends. I just don't know if she'd want you there. You are her *ex-husband*."

"Come on. This is a fund-raiser. I'll pay you double for the ticket."

She thought about it. "Ok, but you did not get this ticket from me!"

It's not just the dancing. Well, okay it is just the dancing. I spend the next two weeks watching You-Tube dance tutorials and practicing the Dougie, the Cupid Shuffle, the Cha Cha Slide, and the Wobble. James Brown, The Temptations, and Gladys Knight and the Pips take me to school.

I repeat to myself, "Slide to the right. Snap. Slide to the left. Snap. Cross. Spin. Snap. Reach out slowly. Pull it back in quick. Snap. Slide to the left. Snap. Slide to the right. Snap."

I lose ten pounds, rent a tux, fill a flask, because I know I'm gonna need it, and I am set. I show up an hour late because I am not getting there before Maya and have another woman all over me with these dance moves. I walk in, spotting her right away. In a room of five hundred, she stands out, not only because she is one of only five white people in the whole room, but because she's beautiful, and she's my wife. No matter what she says, she's still my wife. I take a detour to the bathroom where I down part of the flask before approaching her. She's sitting at the table laughing, picking over her plate. I give the band the nod, and they start playing "End of the Road."

I take a deep breath and say a prayer, coming at her from behind, whispering in her ear, "May I have this dance?"

She turns and looks at me, and I am scared to death. "Oh my God! What? I… I can't believe you're here. What are you doing?" She starts laughing, her face as red as the crimson tablecloth. She takes my hand, and I lead her to the dance floor.

"What are you doing here?"

"I knew *you'd* be here." I catch her eye and for a few moments I feel her heart. Then she speaks.

"You know, this is *my* night with my friends. I can't be responsible for your good time."

"Oh, I'm gonna have a good time, and you're right. You're not responsible for me. You've done that for too long." The closer the song gets to the end, the faster my heart races.

"Are you ok?" she asks. The song is almost over. I take a few steps back, giving the band the nod once again. I'm ready. It's now or never. I might never have this chance again. The moment is right, and the band is *good*. Suddenly I wish I had downed the entire flask.

I start lip syncing to "Ain't Too Proud to Beg," and that's the truth. Just like one of The Temptations, I'm singing, sliding across the floor like I'm on Soul Train. David Ruffin has possessed my body, and I'm all in. One hundred percent committed. All eyes are on me. People start gathering around, clapping. I know the whole routine by heart. She stands watching and laughing, hands covering her mouth. She's completely shocked. I don't have to compete for space on the dance floor because everyone respects a man who's willing to make a fool of himself for a woman. The rest of the world disappears until the last note, when the whole room erupts in applause. We have a great time, a truly great evening. We dance all night, and it's fun, like it should've always been.

I walk her to her car, and a couple of young women speak as they pass. "Y'all were so cute together out there doing y'all's own little thing."

"Thanks," I laugh, and then I look at Maya, "I thought we were doin' the same thing they were doin'."

She starts to fidget with her keys, and just as I start thinking she wants me to kiss her she says, "You shouldn't have come."

"Are you kidding me? We had a great time. Why would you say that?"

"Levi, this is *my* world. I moved to Alljoy to start

over, not to go backwards. I just don't think I can do this. You had your chance. You're an amazing man. I know that some woman is going to be sooo lucky to have you. It's just not going to be me, and I don't want to be mean. I don't want to hurt you, but if I don't tell you these things I'm afraid you're going to get hurt worse in the long run. I'm always going to love you, but I'm not doing this again."

I backed off, but I stayed in Alljoy, having nothing to return to. We shared custody of Fletch, and I realized how much I had missed. It was enough to keep me there, even without her.

A few years had passed, and she called to tell me she needed my help. I could barely understand her through the sobs. She wouldn't tell me what was going on over the phone. I found her on the sofa, wrapped in a purple bathrobe, crying. It looked like she hadn't showered or eaten in days. She was sick, really sick, and she was scared.

She had gone back to have the yellow ink in her tattoo brightened, and days later went for a drunken late night swim in the river, the water leaving her infected with necrotizing fasciitis, a flesh-eating bacteria that had begun to consume parts of her. Dead tissue had to be painfully cut away. Every flower in her tattoo had been infected. By the time she called me, doctors had already removed large pieces of decaying flesh, leaving behind a tree that appeared to be withered and dying. The egg was the last part of the tattoo to become infected. We watched as the symbol of the future began to die, turning a purplish red at first and then black. It had to be cut from the center of her back, leaving an ominous hole.

I held her as she sobbed. Broken and empty, and I couldn't help feeling responsible. Her body wracked by strong antibiotics that only made her feel sicker. Doctors used skin grafts to piece her back together like a patchwork quilt.

"I'm so sorry. I'm so sorry that our lives turned out like this," she said.

"Both of us made mistakes."

"I never meant to hurt you. I just couldn't do it anymore."

"I know. It's ok. I should've never gone to Guyana. I should've listened to you all those years."

I would never wish such a horror on anyone, especially Maya, and if I could've taken it from her I would have. I would have sucked the poison right out of her body and into my own, gladly bearing every scar to save her. It was the only time she ever let down her guard. It felt like a chance to atone for the years I hadn't been there, and I was thankful for the opportunity to love her. She made it clear that I owed her nothing, but all I'd ever wanted was a chance to take care of her, to show her what she meant to me. I learned that truly loving someone meant that I didn't need anything in return.

We spent hours lying in bed, getting high off Cannabis Candy. Trying every flavor lollipop and gummy bear they offered while we watched all five seasons of *Breaking Bad*. I tried to convince her that she had nothing to lose by starting a meth lab. It would be completely understandable. I would be her Jesse Pinkman. There were days that we laughed and days that we cried. I watched her sleep at night. It made me feel homesick, like she was home. I loved her. I would always love her.

Eventually she started to get stronger, her color returning to normal. She felt better until she stood in front of the mirror, looking back over her shoulder at all of the scars and the barren tree. "It's dead," she said as tears ran down her face.

"It's not dead. It's just dormant, and someday God will make you whole again, and you will bloom in colors you never even knew existed. You're still beautiful. There's so much more to you." I hugged her and held her as she cried.

Once she didn't need me any longer, she pushed me away again, insisting that we go back to our separate lives. After a year of caring for her, the thought of searching for gold in Guyana seemed empty and pointless, but it was all I knew. It had been five years of pursuit and rejection. Five years couldn't undo fifteen, and I didn't know if any amount of time would ever truly heal the wounds she carried inside. Fletch was grown and had gone off to college. I never gave up hope, but I had to leave for myself. It wasn't enough to be her crutch when she thought she needed me. I wanted her heart. Returning to the only other home I had ever known, Guyana, I decided maybe if I gave her some space, she would realize why I had pursued her.

And now she was dead in the bottom of some pool on some mysterious island. My wife. Murdered. I should've stayed. I should've tried harder.

Hold on, before I slip away. The flame's gone dark. I am afraid. How strong is flesh and blood? I cannot take back what I've done to you, my sweetest friend. I betrayed you. I walked away again. Now all that's left is what might have been.

- Josh Garrels

8

Simone

My mama always told me I didn't need no man, but we all knew that was a lie 'cause every time the rent was due or the water was 'bout to be turned off, she had a "friend" come visit. There was six of us livin' in a small run down two-bedroom apartment on the South side of Gary, Indiana. Mama would lock the door and we'd all be stuck in the next room listenin', not 'cause we wanted to, but because wasn't nothin' else to hear. There wasn't no headboard, but the bed frame would start bangin' 'gainst the wall. We'd all look at each other, trying to ignore it until one of us would start giggling. One day we was sittin' there half sickishly enduring the bedframe 'bout to make wood chips outta the cheap paneling, when my brother jumped up, started doin' da Wop to the beat. Lord, we laughed so hard, and we jumped up and joined in, a celebration that we wasn't gonna have to beg the neighbors to let us fill up buckets of water just so we could flush the toilet 'til mama could hustle enough money to get the water turned back on.

Our family had two things goin' for it, love and music. Even when we didn't have a radio, we still had a song in our soul. We made our own music. We was born with rhythm, and we learned the blues. Mama raised us on the Supremes, Four Tops, Jackson 5, Marvin Gaye, Stevie Wonder and The Temptations. Each time Mama got pregnant we felt her stomach and swore our little sister or brother was already kickin' to the beat of whatever was playin'. Music saved us. When everything else was falling apart around us, we sang. When we didn't have food, we sang. When our dads ran out on us, we sang. When men put their hands on us after they was done with Mama, we sang. When we was in despair, we sang. Music gave us life and hope and dreams. We pretended we was on *Showtime at the Apollo* with Sinbad or *Soul Train* with Don Cornelius. We was stars, rich and famous; our living room became our stage, each voice in perfect harmony like the Harlem Gospel Choir. We danced and sang our days away.

We raised each other. We was tight. Sleeping in the same bed with four siblings will do that. We didn't have nothin' but each other. There wasn't no money for weaves or perms or make-up or even clothes, for that matter. My sister, the only one older than me, did my hair, sittin' me down in between her legs as she jerked my head back, slicing the sharp end of the comb through my tangled mess of hair. I'd scream, and she'd just carry on with her song, pushing my head forward as she finished braidin' that row, twisting a rubber band in the ends just to make sure she wasn't gonna have to mess with it for at least another week, and then jerking my head back to start on the next row.

When we wasn't pretending we was stars, we played outside in the street, kicking cans and drawing on the road with chalk we'd pocketed at school while the teacher wasn't looking. In the summer Mama would lock us out, tell us to play outside. I got dark. Kids made fun of my blue black skin and my too big, worn out, hand-me-down clothes. All that time, I never thought of myself as pretty, but it didn't really matter none 'cause with all those men comin' 'round to help pay the bills, I wasn't tryin' to look pretty for nobody. I just as soon become invisible.

Mama did what she had to do to survive and to take care of us. Mama had always been an artist, when she had time. Every July we lined up at the Salvation Army for our back to school shopping, each of us leaving with a new book bag filled with supplies. Mama would take a lined composition book to use as her new sketchpad, and she'd draw everything. I'd beg her, "Draw me, Mama! Draw me! Draw me!" And she would. I'd sit for what seemed like an hour, and when she was done, I'd take it to my room and stare at it, tracing my fingers over the lips and cheeks, tracing the outline of my hair. She'd tell us stories and illustrate them. We'd decorate our walls with our names written in graffiti. It seemed anytime she was stressed, which was often, she'd escape into the make-believe world that she created in her sketchpad.

Once she had dated a man named Marcus who moved in after just a couple of weeks. He was a tattoo artist with his own tattoo gun. He set up shop in our apartment, and clients came and went for months. Mama watched, fascinated as he carved his art into the flesh of clients. Finally, he let her give it a try, first on an orange, and then on his shoulder, a pair of hands, praying. I watched silently, knowing not to break her concentration as the ink penetrated his skin, bringing the hands to life, more than life. Next she tattooed the words "Only God can judge" in beautiful script on his forearm, perfect, like something you might see on a fancy invitation.

It turned out it wasn't only God who could judge. One day Marcus was gone, locked up for ten years kind of gone, and all that was left was a tattoo gun and Mama's future. That was the beginning of a new life. She began tattooing on a few friends for tips. Word quickly got around until she was doing tattoo parties in the apartments in Chatham Park. She'd take us with her, in good weather telling us to play outside, and in colder weather telling us to sit still while she tattooed the breasts of big women and the shoulders of men whose muscles was carved like statues. She made good money, and we was happy to not be hungry.

My senior year in high school a Navy recruiter came to my school, promisin' me a ticket out. I saw the way he looked at me, telling me how I would get to travel and experience new things, all the while, his eyes was mapping out my body like he was Christopher Columbus and I was the new world or somethin'. He wasn't bad lookin' neither. That's for sure. It all sounded too good to be true, getting paid to travel, getting out of Gary. I'd live on base, and I'd never have to worry 'bout rent or food or water or power. It was all included, and my paycheck would be mine to spend on whatever I wanted. I leaned in, slowly reaching my hand deep into his pants pocket, searching for a pen, and I signed on the dotted line. We celebrated together in the back of his Ford Explorer.

The military was everything he said it would be. I spent ten years experiencing things I'd only ever dreamed of as I passed by the neglected *National Geographic* magazines in the school library. I traveled to Europe and to the Middle East. I handed out food and water to refugees in Kosovo, and they reminded me of me. I sang my song, my story of blues and my gospel of hope, bridging the space between languages. My strong voice, raspy and deep, my gift to give, comforted the weary in ways that could only be measured in the silence and the stillness that carried my song.

After ten years, I was ready to do me. I moved into a tiny apartment in Midtown Memphis. After a lifetime of cornrows and hand-me-downs, and ten more years of sweats and uniforms, and my hair pulled back in two braids just like Oprah when she played Sethe in *Beloved*, I didn't know how to dress or fix my hair like a real woman. I found a salon down on Beale Street and walked inside.

"Lord, what do we have here?"

I told her I'd never permed my hair before, never really done nothin' to it. "This is gonna be somethin'. You must be from the *coun-try*."

I laughed. "Indiana and then ten years in the Navy."

"So how you end up in Memphis?"

"I'm gonna be a singer."

"All right now. That's what I'm talkin' 'bout. Let's hear what you got, girl. Go on."

Right there in the chair, half my head unbraided into a wild afro, the other side still cinched tight to my head, I closed my eyes and began singing, "A Change is

Gonna Come" by Sam Cooke. The gossip faded and the movement ceased as my voice filled the room. When I stopped everyone in the room was cheering for me. "I don't know," I giggled. "That's just a little somethin'."

"Girl, that's not a little somethin'. Great, Jesus. Well, now I know exactly what to do wid' ya' hair. You trust me?"

I nodded my head and closed my eyes, letting her wash my hair. I'd never been to a real salon before. She began cutting away at my hair, leaving only about six or seven inches. Then she added some violet mahogany hair color to the ends. She braided my hair back into cornrows, setting me under the dryer for a bit. When it was almost dry, she undid the whole thing, leaving it loose and nappy. Then she braided up the sides into a frohawk. She walked away, and I stared at myself in the mirror, turning my face from side to side, squinting my eyes, puckering my lips, trying on the new me. It was like in that one song she got it. *This*, was me. She came back with a light purple dahlia that she had pulled from a vase of fresh flowers. She used her scissors to trim the end, sticking it in my hair, right where the braids and the afro met.

She took a long look at me. Shaking her head, she removed the giant gold hoop earrings outta her very own ears. She dabbed a cotton ball in some blue solution and wiped the posts clean.

"May I?" She looked at me in the mirror, and I nodded my head as she pushed the posts through the holes in my ears and snapped them closed in the other end of the hoop. "Now, you're ready. Get yourself a little black dress and some red lipstick. Go to The Jazz Corner tonight and ask for Ray. Tell him you're Simone. He'll know you're comin'."

Sure 'nough, she hooked me up. I started singin' back-up for the first few weeks. Then Ray booked other women to open for me. I packed the place out night after night, my first real stage. I'd been singin' at The Jazz Corner for almost a year when I met Tobias. I saw him at the bar, entranced by his flirtatious spirit, his eyes, his smile. I was drawn in, and the first break I got I pretended to need a drink. I also pretended not to notice as he made his way towards me.

"Hey."

"Hey," I said back.

"I'm Tobias, or you can just call me your next husband."

I laughed, "I'm Simone, and I'm not married, never have been."

"I guess that'll make me your first husband then. Girl, I could listen to you sing all day and all night. Where you from?"

"Gary, Indiana."

"Home of the Jackson 5, 'Born to Love You'," he smiled.

"You know I only have a minute before I have to be back on stage. How about I sing something special just for you? What you wanna hear?" I laughed.

He eyed me up and down, shaking his head and taking a deep breath like he couldn't believe how beautiful I was. "Killing Me Softly." I smiled, giddy, too excited to say much. Sometimes men fall for the performer, and then they expect life to be a performance.

Singing is easier than believing that I'm beautiful. When I sing, I feel the room. I feel the gaze of men and women, entranced by my presence, my song, my voice, my moves, the sway of my hips, the way I hold the mic. I feel the soul and the pain of the words as I carry the audience with me. I'm not just a singer. I'm a performer.

The rest of it is like looking in the mirror and seeing myself for the first time, my perfect skin, my full lips, my funky afro, and my curves, realizing God gave me more than just a voice. I carry my confidence without apology, and there is sass and attitude in everything I do, every move, the way I pop my tongue against the roof of my mouth in between words, and the way I squint my eyes and tilt my head as I speak.

The story of struggle and hustle is all around me. It's not new, and it's not different. Learning to love is the only thing that can break this cycle, the one where women in my family break the spirits of good men and settle for the ones who will hand them a little cash when the rent is due. Love comes easy, but it doesn't stick around. Our story like the same tune on repeat, each generation adding a new verse to the same old beat, picking the same kind of man again and again. Strong and hard working, his hands supposed to protect and provide, supposed to help raise up our children and stay by our side, save us from the storm that rages inside, but centuries have taught us that it's better to control than to trust. So we yell and we fight and we cuss when we think he's 'bout to leave. We shut a man down, and he flees for reprieve, but my story's gonna be different.

He comes back to the club again and again. We start talkin'. He finally asks me to dinner after my show one night. He pulls around front to pick me up in his black

Mercedes Coupe. He opens the door for me, and I slide across the leather interior, takin' in the smell while he runs 'round to his side. He gets in and starts to drive and then he stops, still in the parking lot.

"I'm sorry, but I have to kiss you," he says, pullin' me to him. It's like a dream. We break apart, but we both feel it, and I'm surprised we manage to make it out of the parking lot at all.

He takes me to a fancy steakhouse. I order a filet that melts in my mouth, the best steak I've ever had, and I can't help but notice, the most expensive, too.

"So, what you do?" I ask.

"I'm a bankruptcy lawyer."

"Business must be *good*."

He just smiled. "Well, this isn't how I grew up," he laughed. "I grew up poor as dirt on a little island off the coast of South Carolina. We didn't even have electricity until I was about eight years old." I imagined white sandy beaches lined with palm trees and clear blue waters and little huts with thatched roofs.

We traded stories of childhood and growin' up poor, his version of poor much different than mine, his childhood filled with loving memories of family and traditions, my childhood, more like a tragic musical.

All that love in his home equaled itself in loss.

"My mom died when I was fifteen, breast cancer. A year later my brother passed away. He was less than a year older than me, so we was close, like twins almost. He'd gone down to the docks to go fishing the night before and never came home. We all just thought he was with his girl, but the next morning the guys running the ferry found him floating face down in the water. He'd drifted pretty far off. We never knew what happened, never could understand how or why he would've ended up in the water."

"I'm so sorry."

"I spent a long time blamin' myself. I shoulda been there. If I had been, it wouldn't have happened. We always went fishing together, but I decided to stay home that night. Everyone told me it wasn't my fault, but it was like a scar that took years to begin to fade. After high school I left for college in Baton Rouge, and my freshman year a woman I'd been with came up pregnant. She had my first child, a little girl we named Ruby. We got married at the courthouse and tried working together to raise a baby while studying for exams, hustlin', me tryin' to play baseball to keep my scholarship money. There were too many fights and too much heartache. She left after a year, and took Ruby back home to South Carolina where she had her family for support. A couple a years later, divorce papers came in the mail with mini highlighter Post-It notes showin' me where to sign."

I listened to him tell me the stories of six more children he had fathered and a life time of child support due, and I would've thought this man must not have any sense or self control in the whole world, but here he was, a successful lawyer who was taking care of his business. He had paid for three out of his seven kids to go to college and was saving for the last three, two was still in middle school and one was still in elementary school.

"My only son, Cameron was a junior, the star running back of his high school, who had been getting calls from universities in the Southeast offering him full rides, when he suffered a severe heart attack during a summer football camp. His life ended, right there on the field."

I felt Tobias's heart. I felt his loss, and I admired his strength. He had manned up, and he took care of his kids. He was smart and charming and charismatic.

He sent me flowers. He took me to Tyler Perry plays, Redbirds' baseball games in the spring and Titans' football games in the fall. We went to concerts and ate out at fancy restaurants. He came to the Jazz Corner every weekend to watch me sing. I was his. He had my heart.

We was married a year later with number eight on the way, a daughter, Nora. Life was good. He was a lawyer, and me, I was livin' my dream as a singer. I stayed home with Nora during the day while he worked, and he kept her in the evenings while I sang. We went on like that for about three years, and then the call came. Tobias's father was diagnosed with ALS. There was no conversation. He quit his job and packed up our lives to move back to the island. Just like that, the life we had known was over.

"You have brothers and sisters. Why can't they take care of him?"

"I can't believe you're asking me that question. Do you have any idea how many people I've lost in my life? This is my father we're talking about!"

"But you didn't even ask me!"

"I don't have to ask you. You're my wife. You go where I go!"

We moved into his father's two bedroom house that couldn't have been more than a thousand square feet. Lead paint shed from the painted trim work inside and outside. For God's sake, we had a baby. Tobias and I shared a double bed with a playpen at the end. Nora had always slept in the bed with us, but there was no room. She spent half the night cryin', tryin' to crawl her way out for 'bout the first month. We woke up early to roosters crowin' and no jobs. Tobias would head out to go fishin' without so much as a word. I'd wake up and try to fix coffee and breakfast while keeping my child away from the window sills, which usually involved stickin' her back in the playpen, where she screamed and cried 'til I was done. For me to shower or get ready I had to leave her in her tiny prison just to keep her safe.

Tobias took a minimum wage job for USCB cleaning up after college kids. My husband, the successful bankruptcy lawyer, was working as a janitor. He assured me that it was temporary. I took care of his father, feedin' him, cleanin' him, all the while Nora was stuck in her little box. When I wasn't taking care of his father, I was 'sposed to be workin' in the garden, weedin' it or pickin' the food and makin' lunch or dinner.

"Nora has been stuck in that stupid playpen for six months!" I'd yell.

"Take her with you. It's a garden, in a yard. She needs to be outside. That's what kids on Goethe do. They play outside. This place is heaven for a kid."

"I feel like some kinda slave here. This isn't what I signed up for!"

"Simone, he's my father! He's all I have left. I've already lost my mother."

"Then be here for him! You're not the one taking care of him! I am!" There was no choice though. Tobias had too many kids to provide for, and the second he quit his job, their mamas was callin', threatenin' to have him thrown in jail. He had to sell the Mercedes and the condo just to keep up with the payments while he waited to go to court to have his payments adjusted, and once he wasn't writin' the big checks no more, women started showin' up on the island, droppin' off their daughters for me to raise.

"Here, you can tell yo' man he can take care of his child for a while since he seems to think a hundred dollars a month is enough to raise a kid." At one point there was six of us living in that tiny, run down, two bedroom shack. One of his daughters slept on the sofa, the other one in the chair, Tobias, Nora and me stuck in our tiny bedroom and his father dying in the other room. Tobias had it easy. He just got up and went fishin' every mornin', dropped the fish off for me to clean and cook for everybody, and then he went off to his job, cleanin' up after some spoiled college kids. He sure wasn't doin' any cleanin' at our house. On the weekends he'd take the mornin' ferry to the mainland where he did side jobs for people, bringin' back a couple hundred dollars that he'd hand right over to his babies' mamas when they finally come for their kids.

It was like the song inside of me died. One day I realized I didn't even sing no more 'cause there wasn't nothing to sing 'bout. That same day his father died in my care. There was no way to call Tobias 'cause there ain't no cell service on the island. As hard as the last year had been, I felt like a piece of me died with him that day. He sat upright in his wheelchair, his breathing labored, like a death rattle. No matter how hard the last year had been, no matter that it hadn't been in my plan to give up so much and work day and night to try to keep everything going, my heart dissolved in those final hours. I took Nora over to a neighbor's house and spent the rest of the day holdin' his hand and singin' old hymns. He looked at me with a love that broke me, knowing how I'd complained and yelled at times. I truly loved this man. When Tobias came home I was still singin', still holdin' his hand. Tobias had to pull me off him, and he held me as I wept. "You should've been here! You should've been here." I sobbed. We buried his father in Canaan Cemetery, right beside his mother and his son.

A month later Tobias was still gettin' up and goin' fishing in the morning, cleaning dorms during the day and working on the mainland on the weekends, like nothing' had changed. I felt like I'd lost him. I started packing our things to go back to the city. I didn't ask. He hadn't asked me when he'd packed up our things to come here. He came home to boxes stacked in the corner of every room.

"I'm not going back."

"Tobias, your father is gone."

"I know, but this is my home. This is the life I want for us and for Nora."

"Tobias, you are a lawyer, not a janitor, and I'm a singer, not some farmer."

"I don't care about the money and living in a city. I don't care about all that stuff. That's all it is, is stuff. I feel like I've been workin' like some slave on the mainland, just to pay for everything. When I'm here, when I'm fishing and outside in nature, I don't need anything else."

"What about me? Do you need me?"

"You're not giving this place a chance. I know the last year was hard for you, but there's more to this island than that. Come go fishing with me. Go to the beach. Get to know the sisters on the island. They don't just sit in their homes shelling peas all alone. This life is about being together."

"That's just it, Tobias. It's about being together, and

we can't be together when you're never here."

"You know I have to work."

"I know you have to work, but not as a janitor, and we don't have to be here to be together. If you get a job as a lawyer you'll make more money, and then we might actually have more time together."

"I work the same hours now as I've always worked. I'm staying."

"That's it? You wasn't even going to talk to me about this? Why would you? You didn't talk to me about moving here in the first place!"

"Give it a chance."

"I'm done giving, Tobias."

The next week Nora and I boarded the ferry and headed to the mainland. Charleston was the nearest city. It was alive with music and performers and art, smaller than Memphis, but with just as much culture and nightlife. I got an apartment and enrolled Nora in preschool. At first we spent weekends commuting. Nora and I would go to the island one weekend and Tobias would come to Charleston the next. It worked for a while, but as I began to book more and more gigs, I needed to be available for the weekends. It worked out okay. I'd drive Nora to catch the Saturday morning ferry to meet her dad on the other side. The ferry captain was Tobias's cousin, and he would let Nora sit in his lap and steer the ship, and then he'd bring her back over on the return ferry Sunday evening. There was no need to go back and forth to Goethe every other weekend, and without Nora, I might not have ever gone back.

We lived our separate lives, remaining married

only on paper, but that was nothing we ever talked about. I wanted my life back. I wanted things to be the way they was supposed to be. I wanted him to move to Charleston with me and get a decent job, and as long as we was still married on paper, I held out hope.

I returned to the island for Tobias's fortieth birthday. I left Nora with some friends in Charleston because I planned to talk to him about moving to the mainland. I packed his favorite strawberry cake, ribeye steaks, potatoes and a little black dress. I knew he'd be gone when I got there. I let myself in and spent the day cleaning the house and decorating.

"What are you doing here? Where's Nora?"

"I left her in Charleston. I thought we could spend some time together, just the two of us. There are things we need to talk about."

"I already have plans. Maybe you should've called first."

"Tobias, look around. Look at all I've done. That's all you have to say?"

"Maybe you should remember that you're the one who left. My life doesn't revolve around whether or not you might unexpectedly show up."

His words was cold, his heart colder. He wouldn't look at me. He showered and left me there. Later that night he eased into the bed next to me.

"Where you been?"

"At The Sandbar with the guys."

"No you wasn't." I knew the lie when I heard it. There was no doubt. He had been with another woman. We both lay there pretending to sleep. Morning came. He pulled on his t-shirt and jeans and told me I should catch the morning ferry. Then he left. I listened to his truck pull down the dirt road, and I began praying, praying and cursing and crying, all of which was indistinguishable.

I knew I'd been unfaithful. There was men in Charleston who, just like Tobias, was drawn by my song, and I was lonely, but I knew in my heart I'd always come back to Tobias. I didn't put too much effort into worrying about Tobias straying because he's related to everyone on Goethe. I understood our situation, and him having something on the side didn't matter to me, but this was different. This wasn't something he was trying to hide. He was pushing me away. This was something deeper, something more. Suddenly I realized I didn't know what he felt in his heart or who I was competin' against. It felt like it might be the end, and that was something I hadn't planned on.

Standin' on the tips of my toes, I reached as far back as I could, feelin' around the top shelf of the closet 'til I found the old cigar box, where he kept the cash from side jobs he picked up on the mainland. Three hundred bucks. I ain't never bought a root before, and I didn't have no clue how much it was gonna cost. I wasn't even sure that I believed, but I wasn't so sure that I didn't either. The folks on the island had as much faith in Dr. Buzzard as they did in God himself and about the same amount of fear, too. People was cautious when it came to talking 'bout him, but stories of roots had been passed on to me as a woman newly married onto the island. Dr. Buzzard was well liked and respected, but you didn't cross him. That's for sure.

Ruth said, "Years ago there was a man from the island named John, and he was laid up in the hospital in

Beaufort. Doctors did everything they could think of, but they couldn't make him better. So they called the family in to say their goodbyes. The family knew it had to be a root, and the only one who can treat a root is a root doctor. So they went and got Dr. Buzzard, bringin' him up to the hospital to remove the curse, and two hours later the man who had just been on his deathbed walked out the hospital on his own and went home."

Martha chimed in, "'Member when 'Lizabeth lost her teeth? She told a lie on her cousin. Next thing, she woke up with an abscessed tooth. She was moaning, in so much pain we had to take her to the mainland where the dentist gave her some medicine to take for a week, and then she had to go back and get her tooth pulled. That happened over and over again, 'bout once a month 'til she'd lost half her teeth. Then one day a stranger came to the island and knocked on her door and said, 'God sent me to tell you there's a root on you, and it's in your pillow. You need to throw that pillow out and then it will stop.' Before she threw out the pillow, she inspected it, pulling off the pillowcase and studying the seams. Sure enough, there was a place where it had been pulled apart and then neatly sewn back together. She tore at the seam with her hands, feeling around inside until she found it, an old piece of dental floss. She burned the pillow and the floss and hasn't had any problems with her teeth since. You can go ask her yourself. She lives right over there by the church."

There was other stories, too. One man got caught cheatin' on his wife, and they say she must've put a root on him 'cause after that he never could get hard again. He tried puttin' moss in his shoes, drinking different rues. He even went to the doctor on the mainland and got a prescription, but nothin' helped. He lost his wife and his mistress. They say he's lucky it didn't just fall off.

"Everybody on Goethe's always so hot 'bout the taxes. Why don't y'all put some root on the tax assessors?" I laughed.

"Root don't work on white people. You ever read *Things Fall Apart*? Just like the missionaries that they put out in the Evil Forest. The Igbos wait for them to die, but nothin' happen to 'em. They wait twenty-eight days. Nothin'. Same thing wid' root. It's 'cause they is the devil, some of 'em."

Everybody on the island knows Dr. Buzzard. People come all the way from the mainland on a regular basis to buy roots or to have roots removed. Real or not, the man was doin' alright for himself. He built the only brick house on the island and owned two Cadillacs. He threw parties, providin' all the liquor and food. The whole island would show up, and Dr. Buzzard was the life of the party, surrounded by women. He'd fathered a bunch a kids on the island, all grown by now. He was known as a good man, helpin' whoever came to him with their problem.

I nervously approached his house, which by all accounts would've looked completely normal if it hadn't been surrounded by all the run down places on Goethe. I walked carefully through the overgrown grass, watchin' my step, afraid I might step on a snake. I knocked on the door and waited.

He walked me out to the oversized barn in the back where he did business, the barn walls covered in shelves that held beakers and bags and boxes of mysteries, all things he used to make potions and spells.

"Oh Jesus, what Tobias do now?" he laughed. "You kumbaya for some joso?" The way he asked made me wonder how many other women had come to him, just like me.

"I don't want you to hurt him. I think he's foolin' 'round."

"You t'ink?" he laughed. He knew.

"How much you got?"

"Three hundred."

"You want her in da' grave, it gonna cost you more dan t'ree hundred. I don't call on da' gafa for less dan a t'ousand, but for t'ree hundred I can give you some root. You put it unda' da' bed, and if another woman sleep in 'da bed, then it'll get 'er. Now what kinda' curse you want?"

"I want something that will leave her so badly scarred that no man would ever want to look at her again."

"You come by tomorrow at dayclean, an' I'll have it for you."

"Thank you."

He smiled, "Of course. Of course. Don't you worry 'bout it now. Dis gonna work. She'll be gone in no time."

The next day Dr. Buzzard handed me a small red bag made of felt that cinched at the top containing a white powder. I took it home, spreading it between the mattress and box springs, and then made the bed. Even if the root didn't work on his side chick, I still had the satisfaction of spending his hard earned three hundred dollars on some white powder, knowing one day he'd look in that box and wonder what had happened. Then I packed my bags and headed back to Charleston without a word.

At some point every human looks right in the eyes of agony and through tragedy asks himself, "How can this happen to me?" You might be the type with enough insight to hold on for your dear life, but slip because your grip is not as tight as you might like. You ain't immune to it, naw, and if you true to yourself then you ain't new to it. Trusted in self, lusted and lured to it.

- Josh Garrels

9

Maya

Life had drained from my body, leaving me like an empty cicada shell desperately clinging to the side of a pine tree in the middle of hurricane season. From outward appearances, I was holding tightly, and from a distance most people didn't notice the hollow shell that I had become. It'd been so many years since I'd played that song of summer that no one even noticed when the music stopped, but a cicada without a song is dead.

I left, sheddin' that old skin faster than a bra at the end of the workday. Freedom's song calling me south, I stretched my broken wings and flew as fast as they could carry me. Finding a new tree, I settled at the edge of paradise, a small fishing village called Alljoy, SC.

I waited for the letter calling me to church discipline, but it never came. Truth was, they probably knew that it'd be easier just to let me go quietly. People'd been called before the session for church discipline for a lot less than a wife leavin' her husband, but all the ones I'd ever seen went humbly before the church, confessin' their ways and turnin' 180 degrees towards a new life. In some sense, I was doing the same, turnin' 180 degrees, but it wasn't towards God, that's for sure.

The shunning began. Friends called to hand down their judgment on how I had managed my life.

"You're completely selfish, narcissistic. You think you do all these great things, helping the kids you teach, but it's nothing more than self-serving charity."

"You're a horrible mother, at best."

"My life is too short for your self-loathing destructiveness of other people's lives, and I'll gladly never speak to you again."

My sin was too ugly, my character too flawed, my madness too toxic. They mercilessly tore the last of me to shreds, and then there was silence. In the silence I could hear God, and he wasn't mad at me. It was okay. I was okay. I was okay because I knew the truth, that I was probably far worse than they could imagine, and I didn't have to get better for God to love me. I understood grace, and there was freedom in that. I chose rejection over oppression and freedom over approval. I just needed to breathe. Ready for something different, I traded the desert for dessert and the manna for honey.

But when you pray for honey, you gotta deal with the bees, too. It wasn't long before TK sunk his hooks deep in my heart. I found my way back to Goethe again and again, first as a volunteer for the Cultural Celebration

Day. The volunteer coordinator put me at the docks on the mainland for the first half of the day with a sign-in sheet. My job was to pass around the clipboard to people who were waiting to board the ferry for the island and have them sign their names.

"I can't write. You gonna have to put an 'X' for my name."

"Oh hell no! This ain't the fuckin' Amistad. I ain't signin' my name to nothin'!"

When the ferry arrived, I was supposed to call out their names and check off the list as they boarded. Between the unfamiliar names and the scribbled handwriting, I struggled, feeling like the kids in school who can hardly read, but for some reason volunteer for the main roll in the class play while all the other kids sigh and moan and begin to roll their eyes.

"What? My handwritin's not good enough for you? You can't read it?"

My face flushed, knowing it wasn't about their names. It was about the color of my skin. Centuries of sins, by my race against theirs, have left their souls scarred, and I reopen the wounds just by being, and the anger l feel in that moment is only a shadow of what they feel. I took each insult, saying nothing; there was nothing to say, nothing to defend. It wasn't my island. I was there in part to pursue another woman's place in another man's heart, and although I may not have been guilty of the sins they assigned to me, I was guilty.

Struggling to keep him as far as possible from my thoughts throughout the day, I prayed for noon to come when my shift would end, and I'd catch the ferry back to the island to enjoy the festival. Twelve o'clock came, and I wandered through the vendors, admiring sweet grass baskets, hand carved wooden spoons and jewelry. I breathed in the smells of pure cocoa butter and soaps scented with citrus and honey. I tasted the sweetness of sugarcane for the first time. Entranced, I watched an older man weave a shuttle over and under lines of cotton to make a cast net that I could only imagine must've weighed a hundred pounds or more wet. Little kids lined up to take their turn. The Ring Shouters danced and sang.

"Maya, hey! You're here!" It was him. I felt as though someone had sucked the air right out of my lungs. "How's your hand?"

I wondered if he could see my heart pounding through my shirt or see the color flood my cheeks.

"It's good. I ummm… I had a great doctor," I said, examining the scars on my fingers.

He took my hand, gently running his fingers over the fine scars. "I'm pretty good with Superglue. So what are you doing here?"

"I volunteered to help."

"You? Volunteered?"

"Yeah. Why not?"

He shook his head, smiling. "Have you eaten lunch yet?"

"No."

"Come on. I think Ajay's got fried fish, ribs and chicken today. You're in luck."

We spent the rest of the day together, talking under the giant moss-covered oaks. The day was coming to an end. School buses filled with tourists headed back to the dock, and I began folding up chairs and carrying them back to the old one room schoolhouse that they now used for storage.

"Shouldn't you catch the bus? The last ferry will be leaving soon."

"I'm staying the night."

"Where?"

"I brought a tent. It's set up… somewhere." I laughed. "I don't know. Someone gave me a ride here in the back of his truck."

"Ok, well, maybe I'll see you. There's usually a party at Samuel's house for all the volunteers. Maybe you'll be there?" I could have stood there for hours just looking at him.

"Yeah, maybe." It turns out that I don't have any game. The only reason I said "maybe" was because I didn't know where I was staying, how I'd get back to my tent, or if I could make it to Samuel's.

Night came, and I found myself drinking moonshine and dancing on someone's porch. I hoped and prayed it was Samuel's. I went outside to cool off. Sparks from a bonfire floated like fireflies, disappearing above my head. I walked out into the middle of the dirt road, away from the people and the noise and stared up at the stars.

"You made it," I heard a familiar voice say.

"I guess so. This must be Samuel's, huh?"

"Yeah, I saw you dancing."

"So why didn't you come dance with me?"

"I like watching you. You're different."

"What do you mean?"

"How many white people do you see here?"

"There *are* actually a handful of white people here."

"USCB kids. They live here. They're interns. How many white people do you see volunteering for Cultural Celebration Day?"

"Counting me?" We both laughed. "Ok, so I'm white. Why does that matter?"

"It's not that you're white. It's that you're here on Goethe, volunteering and dancing and standing in the middle of the road like some kind of dream."

"What about you?" I asked, pretending not to have noticed his wedding band the last time, the one he was no longer wearing. I wondered if he'd tell the truth.

"I live here," he said.

"I know you *live* here. Are you married? Do you have kids?"

"Married. Eight kids. It's complicated."

"Eight kids! Great Jesus!"

He laughed. "You don't have to say it like that!"

"I'm sorry. That's just a lot of kids. All by the same woman?"

"Hell no," he smiled. "I told you. It's complicated. My wife doesn't live here. She lives in Charleston with our daughter. I'm not even sure why we're even married. What about you?"

"I just moved to a town called Alljoy about an hour from here. I have a son named Fletch."

"What about your husband?"

"He lives in South America. I think."

"What you mean 'you think'?" he laughed. "You don't know what country he lives in?"

"It's complicated."

We spent the next few hours sitting by the bonfire weaving our hearts together until we were the only ones left. The music had stopped and the fire was slowly dying.

"Why don't I give you a ride back to your tent?"

"Ok," I said, realizing I had no idea where my tent was. I tried to give directions in the dark. "Turn here, no wait, there. I don't know. That tree looks kind of like the other tree." After riding around for fifteen minutes, I had no clue where I was, much less where my tent was. He drove to his house and turned off the engine.

"Stay with me." He opened the door to his truck, and I followed him inside, thinking back to the first time I was there.

"Oh no. You already got what, eight, nine kids?"

He laughed. "Oh ok, you gonna sleep outside but you don't know where your tent is? You know we got spirits and alligators and rattlesnakes and wild boar on the island, but if you think it's safer than stayin' with me? Go ahead then."

"I'm just kiddin'."

"Nothing will happen. I'll sleep on the sofa."

"It's not you I'm worried about." I smiled as I closed the door to his room, and lay on his neatly made bed. It had been a long hard day. Exhausted, I couldn't think of anything better than sleeping in his bed. I pulled back the covers and slipped beneath the sheets, closing my eyes, imagining him beside me.

The smell of fresh brewed coffee woke me from my sleep early the next morning. I slipped on my jeans, fixed myself a cup and headed out to breathe in the morning air. I walked around the yard, taking it all in. The screen door slammed shut.

"Morning. How'd you sleep?"

"Good. Thanks for letting me stay here."

"Why don't I take you back to your tent where all of your things are so you can get cleaned up? Or you're welcome to bring your stuff back here. There's a shower in the Community Center, and they're having breakfast for all the volunteers. I could come get you in about an hour and show you around the island."

"How'd you figure out where I'm staying?"

He smiled, "The volunteers always stay at the Community Center."

My soul felt a connection to the island, to the people, separate from TK. He came as a beautiful surprise, but he was never the reason for my interest in the history or the culture. The plight of the people to protect and preserve their place in the present from opportunistic oppressors felt familiar, like my own story, and I'd never met anyone before who could understand my story. On a scale of pain to joy, they had found a balance that I was searching for. That's what drew me to the island, to the people.

I was an outsider given a temporary visa to ask questions, my favorite thing. My curiosity tempered, my questions tolerated, maybe appreciated by the simple fact that I wanted to know the truth. I had a respect and a reverence for this place. I knew their story was not my own, but something inside of me longed for connection and community. Someday I'd write my own story. Someday I'd find a place of my own.

I returned to the island several times a year for different reasons, to volunteer, to write, to get away. I became somewhat of a regular, people starting to get used to me. I'd stay at The Cottages. The first time Mabel sent Jedidiah to pick me up at the docks I heard him say over his shoulder, "Great, look what I got myself into." I knew what he meant. He meant that he was gettin' in the truck with a white woman. I was someone he didn't know and didn't trust. His granddaughter Jasmine was the first person on the island to act like I wasn't any different than anyone else. Elanda would bring Jasmine with her to clean up after guests checked out of The Cottages, and Jasmine would just start talking up a storm. Even when she was only about three or four she was an old soul with a big personality and an even bigger imagination. Elanda would clean out the fridge, packin' up the beer that guests had left behind, and Jasmine would put both hands on her hips and tap her foot and declare, "I'm gonna drink some a that beer tonight."

Elanda would laugh and say, "Good, you go right on an' do that. Then you just gonna fall asleep. Then I can get some rest too." Jasmine's foot would stop tapping, and she would squint her eyes, like she was judging whether or not that was the truth. She looked like she probably never wanted to go to sleep, and I imagined she probably wore Elanda out by evening. When it was time to go Jasmine would sit on the bed with her arms crossed, refusing to leave without a fight until Elanda came up with a good enough bribe of an ice-cream sandwich or the promise of seeing a friend. Then she'd hop down, waving bye to me over her shoulder 'til the next time.

All I had to do was show up. He always found me, and the effect of him never lessened, his presence washing over me, renewing my spirit, and it didn't matter if it was minutes or hours. It was always worth it. He taught me how to fish and how to steam oysters. He took me out in the pluff mud to dig for clams.

"There's one right there in front of you."

"Where?"

"Just bend down and feel around with your hand. You'll find it."

I was bent over digging in the mud, all the blood rushing to my head, and I couldn't find anything. I looked back to see him standing there with his arms crossed, checking me out, smiling.

"Oh that's funny," I said, and threw a handful of mud right at him splattering across his chest and face.

"No you didn't," he laughed, throwing a handful of mud back at me. I tried to take off running, slipping in the pluff mud, TK tackling me, both of us laughing, completely covered in mud. I wanted him to kiss me so bad, and the fact that he had never tried confused things. We both jumped to our feet, staring at each other, hearts racing. He smiled. Without saying a word, he wiped some of the mud from my face, away from my eyes.

"We can't get in my truck like this."

"Of course not." I ran into the water and started scrubbing off. He just stood on the shore covered in mud, watching me. I got my clothes as rinsed out as possible and then stripped down to my bathing suit.

"Why didn't you come in and rinse off?"

"I'm not going in that water. You know what's in there?"

"Are you serious?"

"Yes, I'm serious. I don't swim in the ocean."

"Well, I wasn't really swimming. I was more like

standing and washing mud off me."

"No, I am *not* going in there."

"Well that's the craziest thing I ever heard. I guess I'm driving you home then," and I smiled.

He handed over his keys, climbing in the back of the truck. That was the first time I ever drove on the island, the first time someone was forced to trust me with their vehicle.

Each time I came to the island I felt myself falling deeper and deeper for TK. My divorce was final, and I had to tell him. It was the only time that I called to let him know I was coming, just for the day, too unsure of his reaction to plan on staying over night. He picked me up at the dock and took me out to throw the cast net, which I tossed haphazardly, catching it on an oleander bush. He laughed and came over to help me, sensing my nervousness.

He slid behind me, wrapping his arms around my shoulders, and began untangling the net from the branches before me. His breath soft and warm against the back of my neck, "You okay?" he asked. The heat of his body pressed against mine made it impossible to think straight, to speak. Words tumbled from my mouth as my face flushed. I was convinced that it would be my last trip to the island. I would walk back to the dock where I would sit and wait for seven hours until the ferry returned to the mainland.

"I'm in love with you." I waited for the earth to open up and swallow me whole where I would burn alive in the firey mantle, and then he kissed me, and I didn't die.

"Stay the night. I'll be sure you make it on the first ferry back tomorrow. I just wanna be with you."

"I can't…Fletch. I'm not ready for that." He didn't

push. Knowing we had both been there in our hearts and in our minds wouldn't make the reality of going there any easier. It would complicate things, change things. We would wait until we were both ready.

Instead, I came and went from the island with new projects. I started writing a book. A few of the descendants allowed me into their lives, generously sharing their culture and their stories with me. I hoped to produce something that would bring attention to the property tax issue, make it more than just a piece of land to be acquired by the wealthy, and put a face to the people, make them more than a name attached to a plat to be purchased and possessed. The land is the people. It's all the same. To force the sale of one is to sacrifice the other.

Each time I fell more in love with the island and more in love with TK. He shared his stories with me as well, stories of women and children and broken hearts, and love and loss. He had lived, really lived. He had followed his heart, and he had the scars to show for it. My life had been just the opposite, safe, honest, right, true, and for all that, I had the same scars and the same broken heart without any great story to go with it. I saw TK, his heart unlocked and his soul bare, and I knew he would be the one exception, my greatest adventure.

Goethe was like a new world to me, a community of people who knew more about life and love and living than I ever knew there was to know. I learned from watching and listening and just being still. They had a deep connection to their ancestors and to each other. Their ways were based on traditions and stories. The women on the island, the Goethe Sisters, were strong, like me. I watched with wonder as Elanda collected vegetables from her garden, shelled peas while running the store, took care of The Cottages and crocheted a blanket while watching after Jasmine and sharing stories with me. That's how I saw life on the island. It was simple. People worked hard, ate well, loved passionately and lived long.

The Soul Sisters invited me to come down for the weekend to start the sweet potato garden. We would turn the ground, preparing the soil for the first planting.
The sweet potatoes would be used to make beer and whisky and pies and all sorts of things that could be sold to raise money to help people pay their property taxes. Elanda said that if all it took to move a mountain was faith the size of a mustard seed, then surely faith the size of a sweet potato could save Honey Hill. I was in. We'd been working for hours. Miss Lollie, the oldest Soul Sister, who was in her 90s, was too old to be diggin' in the heat of summer, but not too old to walk over a mile to bring us lunch. Sweat dripped from my face and back, my muscles ached, and I'd never felt better.

I knew it was just a matter of time before he would find me. I could feel him, and I searched the distance, across the field. There he was, like a dream. It had been nearly four months since I'd seen him. Without a word, not caring what anyone thought, I dropped my shovel and ran as fast as I could in Elanda's snake boots that were two sizes too big.

"What are you doing here?"

"Diggin'," I smiled. "Wanna work?"

His eyes traveled up and down my body, eyebrows

raised, "Yep."

We spent the last two hours of the day playing more than working. I stopped and watched him, really watched him. He could feel it, stopping and resting his chin on the handle of the shovel, he stared at me. I was ready.

That night we made love for the first time. For a minute my soul felt free from gravity, like I might float to the moon. He sank his hooks deeper and deeper into my soul, tethering my heart to his. Freedom came with new shackles that I pretended were priceless bands of gold.

Every moment we were together, made it harder to be apart, making me want him more. Just the sight of him sent a wave of adrenaline through my body, and the thought of him took my breath, making me drunk with excitement. He made his way into my thoughts during the day and into my dreams at night. I closed my eyes to escape, drifting into other worlds and he was always there, trying to find me. Just as I had begun to feel whole again, I gave pieces of myself away, naively unaware of the consequences.

My heart was on the island. I'd given it to him, freely, believing everything, believing that our love could thrive while other relationships died, that good could come from this, that truth didn't matter as long as I could believe the lie. My soul felt hollow and empty. Once again I found myself waiting on a dream. He'd given me his heart and his body, but it wasn't enough for us to share the most intimate pieces of ourselves without the promise of sharing our lives. I wanted forever. I wanted time with him, but he had given all that he was willing to give. He dreamed aloud of a future that deep down I knew would never happen, a promise that would never come, a time that would never be right.

By the time I stopped believing that it was real, it was too late. My soul had become unsettled. Unraveled. Addicted. Bound. I'd tell myself that I'd never return to the island again, and I wouldn't for a while. I'd ignore his calls, promising myself that it was over.

My birthday came, and I unlocked the door to my classroom, remembering the year that Levi had covered my board with Post-It notes spelling out "I love you" and the beautiful flowers he'd left for me. Leaving the lights off, I sat at my desk, taking in the silence, the stillness, the emptiness, and then I did what I had always done, my job. I turned on the lights and busied myself preparing for students to arrive. The day flew by. Packing up my things, I thought I'd go get myself one of those five dollar cupcakes, the ones with as much icing as cake. I pushed open the door that led to the parking lot, and there he was, TK, leaning on the hood of my car, smiling, waiting for me. That's all it took, all resolve was instantly dissolved in that one look, that look.

"Happy birthday, beautiful. I've missed you!"

"I can't believe you came! You're *here*?"

"Well, somebody won't answer my calls. So I had to do something."

"Oh my God. I can't believe you're *here*."

"It's your birthday. I had to see you." We stood, staring at each other.

Grinning, I shook my head in disbelief and complete wonder. "What are we gonna do?" I asked.

"We're gonna get married." I stood staring at him, ready to go to the courthouse. "But for tonight, I'm gonna take you out, and then I'm going to take you home." His words wound around my soul like a bundle of barbed wire so that every move hurt, whether it was forwards or backwards didn't make any difference. God told me to "be still," but I couldn't, and it hurt just to breathe. He pulled the wire tighter and tighter, the barbs sinking deeper and deeper.

Before he left the next day, he handed me an envelope, a note promising to come for me when the time was right. He wanted me to keep it, to bury it.

"Why do I need to bury it?" I asked.

"Just trust me."

There were days that burying it made perfect sense, days I would've worn it thin reading it again and again, days my tears would have blurred the ink on the pages, days I would have burned it or torn it up. But I knew where it was, proof that it hadn't just been a dream, proof that he felt it too, proof that I wasn't crazy.

His promise was enough to keep me going back for another year, and then another birthday came and went. This time he didn't show. Anxiety started to take over like an earthquake in slow motion. It was happening. The deepest heartache like the earth was splitting open and swallowing me whole until the only thing I wanted more than TK was peace.

I used to imagine being locked up in some mental

ward, and the only way for me to get out was to prove to the doctor that I was telling the truth. I'd take the conch shell, the same one I'd used to bury the note, and I'd dig and dig for hours. Finally, I'd feel the thud of the shell against the Tupperware, and I'd hold up the container, like it was the winning lottery ticket. I'd tell the doctor, "See! I told you! I told you it was real," and then I'd peel off the lid and pull out the notecard. "See!" I'd unfold it only to discover it was completely blank, and then I'd sit on the ground weeping while the doctor explained how I'd become so disconnected with reality that I'd made the whole thing up. Just like Leonardo DiCaprio on *Shutter Island*. Once a year they'd let me act out the whole scenario as part of my therapy so that I could remember the truth just for a day, but it never stuck. There was no TK. There never had been. It had all just been part of my imagination. Then we would bury the note again for the next year.

I pulled at the shackles, unable to free myself. I fell on my face and prayed for freedom.

And then I got sick.

It had been several years since I'd gotten my tattoo. I still loved it as much as the day Levi had first drawn it on me. It was the *one* scar that I had chosen to bear, and it was beautiful. I kept it covered in sunscreen, but years of living at the beach, spending all summer running around in sundresses and tank tops had faded the yellow, turning it nearly the same color as my skin. I looked over my shoulder at the egg, the future, which had faded, nearly disappearing, and I decided to stop by the tattoo parlor. The guy suggested that I have it touched up. It would only take a few minutes, and he'd do it for fifty dollars. He said he'd go ahead and take care of the centers of the flowers too while he was at it. A few days and a few drinks later, I decided to go for a swim in the river.

No decision is as simple as it seems, no choice inconsequential. One by one, each flower began to burn and itch. The flowers held heat like a fever, and my whole body ached. Within days my back looked like it was covered in bruises, every flower purple and swollen. Soon they began to open up, raw and bleeding, oozing with infection that smelled like death, the pain unbearable, and I knew I was in trouble.

The ER doctor said I needed to be admitted for emergency surgery. The anesthesiologist placed the mask over my face, instructing me to take deep breaths, assuring me that I was going to be all right. As I drifted away, Langston Hughes came to me.

"Mr. Hughes," I said. "I know now. I know what happens when a dream is deferred. It becomes a festering sore that oozes and smells like rotting meat.

"Baby, that's 'cause you dreamin' 'bout all the wrong things," he told me.

Struggling to open my eyes, still groggy from the anesthesia, I was remembering the surgery. Trying to make sense of the beeps of IV's and heart monitors, I was lying on my side staring at the wall. I started to roll over, feeling a nurse gently place her hand on my healthy shoulder.

"Don't move. You just got out of surgery. Let me go

get the doctor so he can talk to you."

The doctor came. "You had some extensive surgery done on your back so we have you on your side to keep some of the pressure off your wounds so they can start to heal. The antibiotics will work to get the infection under control, which will also help with the pain. Can you tell me what you remember?"

"My tattoo. It was itching at first. Then it started to get sore. It hurt so bad, like someone had beaten me." I took a breath to keep from crying, "and it smelled, too."

"Did you go swimming after getting your tattoo?"

"A few days later. In the river."

"It appears you contracted a flesh-eating bacteria called necrotizing fasciitis. It destroys the subcutaneous tissues, or the deeper layers of the skin. It can spread quickly. Therefore, it had to be removed right away. You're lucky that we caught it so early."

Tears caught in my throat as the aloneness set in.

As if he could hear my thoughts. "Is there anyone we can call for you?" Fletch was away at college, and I had driven myself to the ER.

"No."

I spent the next three days in and out of consciousness, awakened by beeps and buzzes and nurses changing my bandages. I was hooked to a morphine drip to manage the pain.

Slowly I began sitting up and going to the bathroom on my own. "They are probably going to let you go home tomorrow, but you will have to have someone to help you change the bandages, or we could send a Home

Health Care Nurse."

"It's okay. I know who I can call."

"Let's go ahead and change your dressings while you're sitting up."

She carefully peeled away pieces of tape and gently tugged at the gauze covering the wounds, piece after piece came off. Finally, she began to uncover the front of my shoulder. I looked like the surface of the moon, covered in deep craters with jagged edges.

I felt like someone had turned me inside out, every scar that I had managed to hide now exposed. The dead skin carved out to make way for new life, painful but necessary if I was going to live, which I wasn't so sure about either. As the doctor removed the dead tissue that threatened to take my life, he had also removed the hooks that tethered my heart to TK's and threatened to steal my soul. The wounds would heal slowly, each one leaving its mark forever. The chains were cut, and just like that, I was free, suffering and alone, but free.

TK called again and again, but I couldn't face him. I could barely face myself in the mirror. I didn't believe anyone could ever love me like this.

I called Levi.

He was the first person to see my scars. He told me that I was beautiful as he changed the dressings on my wounds and held me when I felt hopeless. I refused to go anywhere, and Levi refused to let me sit at home. He knew how much I loved the beach, and he offered to take me there, but I couldn't do it. I couldn't face a beach full of beautiful people. "You need to get out, feel the sun on your face, smell the salt air." I just couldn't. So he drove me to the beach at night. We lay in the dunes, wrapped in a warm blanket, listening to the waves and watching the stars. He put his life on hold to take care of me. I'd never been weaker or more helpless.

The sickness, the surgery, the scars had made a shift in my heart's perspective, and I almost forgot about TK, finding God in all the empty spaces that were left. Finding peace. Finding freedom. Becoming whole again. Eventually I was strong enough that I didn't need TK or Levi anymore.

There's so much more to life than we've been told. It's full of beauty that will unfold and shine like you struck gold my wayward son. That dead weight burden weighs a ton. Go down into the river and let it run and wash away all the things you've done. Forgiveness alright.

- Josh Garrels

10

Tobias

I dive beneath the waves, remembering the promise that I had made. She used to beg me, reassuring me that she'd never let anything bad happen to me. She waited, urging me to dive in, deep, and in I had, in more ways than one. If anyone on Goethe saw me they would think I was crazy, swimming way out into the deep waters. I can feel her all around me, pushing me above the surface, forcing air into my lungs, carrying me back to the shore, protecting me. I stand on the beach completely naked and covered in goose bumps as the sun begins to dry my skin and warm my body. I've never felt more alive.

Maya Indigo. The very body that embodied life now lay lifeless in the bottom of a pool. I didn't know what had happened, but it didn't really matter. Knowing wasn't going to bring her back. It wasn't the first great loss I'd known, but it was the first since I had opened myself to feeling again. Part of me regretted loving her, and the other part knew I would be okay. I had experienced greater loss and greater hurt. I'd lost a child, my only son, and once you survive that, there's nothing you can't overcome. Of all of the women in my life, she was the one who stirred my soul, unlocked my heart and inspired deep romance, reminding me of what it meant to live life fully. She taught me to trust my heart again, convincing me to let her in, and her spirit continued to move me just as it had from the very first day we met at the dock. I knew from the first moment I saw her that she was going to be someone special. I could feel it, the pull between us.

I close my eyes and imagine the last time she was here with me. It had rained the whole time. We spent most of the weekend inside, slow dancing to old Marvin Gaye albums.

"See, my folks used to dance to this album, and my dad would spin my mom around and then dip her, just like this."

"Oh yeah," she smiled.

"And we'd sit on the sofa over there and watch, praying they didn't kiss. 'Cause who wants to see a couple old people makin' out? Now I know what they were doing."

"They were just waitin' for y'all to go to bed."

We went fishing in the rain and picked vegetables from the garden, and I taught her how to fry fish. "I'm scared the grease is gonna burn me," she said.

"Girl, you're the most dangerous thing in this kitchen right now," I said as she tossed fish into a hot vat of oil from two feet away. "Come here." I held her from behind as she laughed. "Trust me."

"Is that a question or a statement?"

"Both," I smiled. We ate good food and drank our wine. Then we snuggled up on the sofa, watching Denzel Washington movies and dreaming of the future. It was the middle of the afternoon, and she sat up and looked at me so deliberately.

"What?" I asked.

She blushed, "It's just… I've always," she hesitated.

"Always what?"

Her face grew warmer. "I've always wanted to have sex in the rain."

"Well, that's a really good rain out there. It's actually perfect sex rain."

"Really?" she laughed. "Is there a gauge for that?"

"Well it's warm enough outside that we won't freeze in the rain. It's coming down pretty good, but not too hard. Yep, it's perfect."

She smiled. "Let's do it," and she grabbed my hand, leading me through the house, and out the back, the screen door slamming behind us as we ran through the rain and out into the field behind my house. We ran until we were out of breath, and then she stood, looking at me, smiling. I waited to see what she was going to do. There was something so innocent about everything she did, like everything was new, and I just wanted to watch her experience things for the first time. Every time I would wait, until it was too much for me to hold out any longer. She took the rosary from around my neck and hung it around her own, tucking it inside her tank top which was now soaked and clinging to her body. I watched the outline of the beads between her breasts as they rose and fell with the rhythm of her breathing. She pulled me in, kissing me until I lost myself, my body melting into hers, our spirits becoming one, right there in the middle of the field, both of us covered in grass and dirt. We went back home to wash off and warm up in the shower before she had to catch the ferry home, and then I never saw her again. She just disappeared without any explanation, almost like she had been a dream. There were times that I questioned if any of it had been real or if I had just imagined the whole thing.

I spent two months leaving messages and sending texts. At first I thought something was wrong. She must have lost her phone, and then I began to worry that it was something worse. Maybe something had happened to Fletch or to her parents, and then I was scared something had happened to her. That thought gave way to years of experience with women making manipulative moves to get what they wanted. That was her way of giving me an ultimatum, to show me a great weekend and then to disappear, to let me know I was expendable if she didn't get what she wanted.

None of that made any sense. I went back and forth in my mind. She was different than other women, and I knew that. She didn't play those kinds of games. She just said what she felt. I wanted to be with her so badly. I wanted to spend the rest of my life watching her discover the world, but I'd already been through one divorce, and I knew how costly it would be, financially and emotionally, and as much as I wanted forever with her, I didn't want to miss out on a single day with Nora. I had already buried one child, and had kids from here to New Orleans that I saw once a year for a week, not enough to feel I was truly an influence in their lives. Nora was my heart and my whole world. I spent every moment that Nora and I were together making her feel like the most special person in my life, and no one was going to get in the way of that. A divorce would mean more child support and possibly alimony too, not to mention I knew Simone would use Nora to get back at me. I would never get to see her, hold her, raise her, just another paper daddy to another kid.

If I could make Maya understand, if I could just convince her that when the time was right I would come for her, then I might get both of my worlds. I kept calling until she changed her number. I took the ferry to the mainland and drove to her school where they informed me that she was taking an extended leave of absence. That's all they would say. I knew something had to be wrong. Teaching was her passion. She would never leave it without a good reason.

I sat outside her house for the better part of a day, trying to figure out what it was I wanted, afraid of intruding on her life, afraid of making more promises that I couldn't keep. A man pulled into the driveway, in her car. It was Levi. I recognized him from pictures. He pulled out a bouquet of flowers and bags of groceries, letting himself into her house and closing the door behind him. What had happened? I knew he loved Maya. He had taken her for granted for years, but once he realized what he had lost, he had never stopped pursuing her. I could only assume he must have finally won her heart. She must have made her choice, and she couldn't tell me.

On my way home I thought about Nora and Simone. Maybe it hadn't been fair of me to expect her to give up her whole life without so much as the consideration of a conversation. She had come to the island, and she had spent a year caring for my father when I couldn't. She had loved him through his last days and minutes. She had raised our daughter and done her best at caring for my other girls, too, when their mamas would get fed up, dropping them off like she was some kind of *Nanny 911*. Taking the evening ferry back to Goethe, I drove home and went to sleep, and I dreamed of Maya, night after night.

Simone was smart and beautiful and talented, but she wasn't Maya. Maya Indigo had changed me. She had moved my heart and my soul. She had managed to do what no other woman could. Now she was gone. She was nowhere and everywhere at the same time, and I was lost without her, lost and found. She was at the dock where I fished in the morning. She was where I threw cast nets in the evening. She was at the Community Center and the GIPS's office and The Sandbar, and The Cottages and at Elanda's house and in the sweet potato patch and at the beach and walking down the dirt roads. I knew what I had always felt was true. Our spirits were connected, our lives meant to intersect for the time that they had.

Long days turned to weeks and months, and I found myself in the same routine, cleaning dorms, fishing, gardening and picking up side jobs. I went through the motions. Maya had my heart, and I gave away the last pieces of my soul to women from the mainland who stopped by for servicing. Every experience, every act, felt empty. Maya had given me more, made me want more.

I went for a walk and found myself in the cemetery, the one place where I'd never been with Maya. It was a place where I could talk to the spirits. I lay on the ground between my mother and my son and looked up at the bluest sky through the moss-covered branches of the oak trees. It had always been a place where I felt rooted, a place where I could hear the wisdom of the ancestors. I fell asleep, and in my dream my mama came to me, laying down beside me in the grass, staring up at the clouds as they changed into different animals.

"Mama, what do I do?"

"Time will heal your heart. Baby, you've loved many women in your life," she laughed, "and you'll probably love many more, but family is always the most important thing. A family that's united eats from the same plate. You got a baby in Charleston who needs you. You gotta get your family back together, son."

I woke up and lay staring up at the sky, praying for peace. I began cleaning up the cemetery, gathering small branches that had fallen from the trees and tossing them beyond the fence. I picked up pieces of broken dishes, brushing away dirt and leaves, carefully placing them back on their graves.

I missed Nora. I knew that when I went to Simone I better have something to show, something to prove that I was willing to change, willing to make it work. I put on my best suit and spent the next week passing out resumes to law firms all over Charleston. Three called me back and offered me interviews. I found my place working part time for a non-profit Civil Rights firm that had been handling some of the tax appeals of descendants on my island. I told them about my family's personal experience, how our taxes had gone from a couple hundred dollars to over two thousand dollars in one year. I told them about one lot on the island that had gone underwater a long time ago, and was still assessed at a quarter of a million dollars. It seemed as though no one had ever even come out to see this piece of property before estimating its value. They were interested in having a descendant who had personal knowledge of the inside issues and politics. It wouldn't pay much, but otherwise it was a perfect fit.

After securing the job, I called Simone and asked if I could take her to dinner after her gig. Arriving at the club, I listened to her soulful voice carry the room, and knew she could have any man she wanted. I felt the thirsty room looking at her like a vine of grapes growing on the side of the road, but she was only looking at me. She was wearing the little black dress she had worn the first night I heard her, her hair braided up into a frohawk with a purple dahlia tucked behind her ear. That was my wife, and she was beautiful, inside and out. I closed my eyes, her voice taking me back to when I had fallen in love with her at The Jazz Corner in Midtown Memphis. Between the pressure of work, losing my father and always dealing with child support that was never enough, my vision had become blurred, and I had given up. My mama used to say it was easier to fall in love than it was to stay in love. I knew I'd put all my effort into work, and nothing into my marriage.

Maya Indigo had awakened my soul with a love as pure and sweet as raw sugar. She reminded me of what it meant to feel like morning. She taught me what it meant to chase a woman's heart. She showed me how to listen and actually hear, how to look and truly see. She would always be part of me, and I prayed that wherever she was, she was happy.

I opened my eyes and saw my wife. I thought about her and Nora picking cucumbers and tomatoes in the garden, and I imagined her singing to my father and holding his hand as he passed away. I owed it to her to see if there could really be anything left between us. I guessed the news of working for a non-profit would show me where we stood.

"So?" she looked at me untrustingly.

"You look beautiful." I looked at her, and it was as if I was seeing her for the first time.

We stared at each other for a while. "You too," she said.

"I miss you."

"Tobias, what you here for?" she said, sucking her teeth and squinting her eyes at me. "Don't be asking me if you can skip paying me. I know we're not divorced and it's nice of you to send a check every month to help out, but the bills don't stop just 'cause of your other kids. Nora's in dance and that money helps us make it here."

"I got a job working for a firm here in Charleston. I'm going to be representing the tax appeal cases of the descendants."

"You got a job? Working for a law firm? Here in Charleston?"

"Well, it's a non-profit, and it's just part time for now, but you know part time for a law firm is like full time for any other job." Before I could finish she grabbed me in a hug. I could feel her chest heave with emotion as she tried not to cry. "I can work from home, or I can stay here some if you want. Maybe we could go back and forth between our homes." I pulled her off me. I wanted her to see me. I wanted to know that she heard me. "You know I only got this job to be near you." Tears flooded her face, and I wiped them away. "Or I could get my own place."

She started laughing. "You are *not* getting your own place."

"I'm not going to make that much money, and I'm not going to work all the time. We're not going to be driving a Mercedes and eating out all the time."

She buried her face in my neck. She was warmer than I had remembered. "Tobias, you are all I have ever wanted. The money never mattered. I thought I had lost you."

"Let's take it slow, okay?"

"Okay," she said, nodding in agreement.

"Well, I asked you to dinner. Didn't I?" I pulled around in my '94 Nissan Maxima, a used car I'd picked up for getting around on the mainland. I jumped out and opened the door. "It's not the Mercedes."

"Tobias, I never loved you because of a car or a job. I just wanted you."

I knew that we were going to be okay. I reached over and kissed her, softer than I'd remembered. We went to dinner at IHOP, laughing and talking over pancakes for an hour, flirting like we was in high school. Afterwards I took her home.

Nora was asleep in the bed. We paid the baby sitter.

"Can I see her?"

"Of course, Tobias. She's yours."

Simone walked away, giving me a moment with my

little girl. The first thing I noticed were the purple walls, her favorite color. I tiptoed across the floor and sank down to my knees beside her bed. Overcome with emotion, it was the first time I had cried in years. I had been a fool to risk losing a minute. She was my heart and my life. I looked at her sweet face, the perfect combination of Simone and me, her flawless skin the color of creamy cocoa and caramel kisses, her wild hair tied away from her face with a purple paisley headband. I scooped her up in my arms. Without waking up she put her arms around me, resting her head on my shoulder, and I thanked God that I hadn't lost this chance to be a father. "My Girl" began playing from the other room, and I could hear Simone sing as she put away dishes and straightened things up. I danced and sang to my little girl and then tucked her back in the bed.

I walked back into the kitchen and picked up a dishtowel and started drying the dishes and putting them away.

"That's probably the sexiest thing I've ever seen you do," Simone laughed.

"Oh yeah, wait 'til you see me cook breakfast."

"Oh, I guess you're staying then." She smiled.

"I guess so."

The next morning I snuck into Nora's room and woke her up. "Daddy! Daddy! Daddy!", the sweetest words I've ever heard. I picked up my little girl and spun her around, then kissed her all over as she giggled and squealed. I watched her dance and listened to her tell me stories. I made the most of every moment.

We went back and forth between the mainland and

the island. We didn't have much. Life on the island kept us balanced, connecting us to our roots, reminding us that what little we had was more than enough. We found contentment and peace, and life was good.

Trouble has beset my ways and wicked winds have blown. Sirens call my name, say they'll ease my pain. Then break me on the stones, but true love is the burden that will carry me back home. Carry me with the memories of the beauty I have known.

- Josh Garrels

11

Maya finds her new orbit, one with enough gravity to keep her from spinning out of control and enough space to allow her to dance freely. She finishes the book, a love story set on Goethe. She packs an overnight bag and boards the evening ferry to take her manuscript to the island, hoping to receive a blessing. Jedidiah picks her up and drives her to The Cottages where Mabel is waiting. Rather than sitting around fretting over what Mabel might think, she throws some moonshine and mango chips in a bag and borrows a bike to ride to the beach. Taking the cut through the woods to the sweet potato patch, she stops, finding herself more moved by the memories than she had expected. Laying the bike down, she walks to the spot, and starts to dig up the note with her flip-flop, an impossible task. She quickly gives up, reminding herself that isn't why she came to the island. She rides the rest of the way through the woods to the beach, walking her bike past the dunes and down to the water. Riding along the edge, she cuts the surf with her front tire, sending up a spray of salt water on either side.

Just as she approaches the pavilion she sees him, his silhouette against the sunset, holding hands with a woman, a young girl dancing back and forth in between them. Maya freezes. He picks up the little girl, spinning her around in circles. He puts her down and then he leans in, kissing the other woman just the way he used to kiss Maya. Ducking down into the dunes, feeling embarrassed and exposed, she prays that a tsunami washes her away. Maya had never even thought of him waiting for her after she cut things off so abruptly, or wanting her now that she was so terribly scarred, but seeing him with his wife tears at the old wounds, painfully opening her up all over again. She feels weak. A voice, soft as a whisper says, "You were never enough."

Doing the only thing she knows to do, she pulls the moonshine from her bag and tries to disappear. She watches as the family enjoys the sunset, and then they leave. She wonders if the whole thing had been a lie, if she had ever meant anything to him, if she had lost everything for nothing. What if she were just a patient who'd escaped from the insane asylum and made the whole thing up? Suddenly, between the grief and the moonshine, anxiety overwhelms her just like that dream, the one where she has to dig up the note to prove that it had been real. She finds a conch shell and sticks it in her bag, heading back down the beach in the dark.

Maya stumbles blindly, half drunk, down the path towards the sweet potato patch, back to where it all began. Tears burn her eyes. She smells the sandy soil, and falls to her knees, crawling to the exact spot where they first made love. She can feel it. He was only the second man she had ever let inside her body, and the first man she had ever let inside her heart. He had waited years for her, waited and watched, not wanting to interfere in her life, not wanting to lead her down a path that he knew would cause a lot of pain. It was Maya who had made the first move, telling him that she was in love with him, and it was Maya who had whispered in his ear that day as they were working in the sweet potato patch that she was ready. The pain in her soul and the smell of the rich dirt are her only proof that she's still breathing and still in this world. Everything else is a dream.

The sweet potato patch was just being born out of an idea back then. She had come to the island for the weekend to help turn the soil and plant the new garden to start *Yam Bam Spirits*. She had hoped he would find her, and when he heard she was on the island, he couldn't resist. He stood off in the distance taking all of her in before she realized he was there. There she was, covered in dirt, sweat dripping down her face and arms leaving behind the only clean streaks on her body. Smiling at the site of her LSU tank top, running shorts and snake boots up to her knees, all he could think was she had never looked more beautiful. That was the woman he was going to marry. As if she could feel his stare, she turned and searched the horizon, laying down her shovel and shading her eyes. As soon as she saw him she took off running across the garden and tackled him right there in the dirt. That got all the sisters talking. He was the finest man on Goethe, with a long history of women on and off the island, and one thing was for sure, he wasn't Maya's husband, and she wasn't his wife, but no one said anything. Everybody knew how Simone had taken his baby and left the island, and everybody also knew Tobias wasn't the faithful kind.

She didn't call him Tobias, like everybody else. She called him TK. He rolled up his pants and worked all afternoon in the sweet potato patch. The sisters kept giving each other the wink and the nod, eyeing his calves, just waiting for him to get hot enough to take off his shirt, but Maya and TK were oblivious, like they were the only two people on the whole island. She'd stand right in front of him and bend way down to sift through the overturned soil, looking over her shoulder and giggling at him. Her face would turn red hot, and the back of his head would get all giddy. Before long they were throwing acorns and chasing each other around. They didn't pay any mind to anyone. He had been half kidding when he whispered in her ear, "I just want to take you right now, right here in the sweet potato patch."

He was shocked when she looked at him and said, "I think I'm ready." She had only been with one man in her whole life, her husband, waiting until her wedding night to have sex for the first time. He never expected that she would cross that line with him. It wasn't until later that night after dinner that they wandered back to the sweet potato patch to make love for the first time under the full moon. She soaked in the site of his smooth skin, dark and rich like coffee, she drank it all in. He held her with his eyes,

eyes that exasperate and captivate, hypnotize and mesmerize. Strong arms that used to hold her in her dreams, held her like a dream so that she couldn't tell if she was awake or asleep. Beautiful calves and thighs, he thrust his way inside of her. One soft touch from his hard working hands, and she melted like moonlight across the May River on a warm summer night. That's how they spent the night, making love on a blanket in the middle of the garden, their Eden. They stayed in the sweet potato patch until almost morning, getting up just in time to wander hand in hand down to the beach to see the sunrise.

The sweet potato patch wasn't grown up back then like it is now, but even in the thick of the vegetation, her heart tells her when she has reached the spot. She takes the conch shell from her bag and begins to dig down into the earth. She had buried it deep because she knew the soil would be tilled again and again year after year. She digs until she feels the shell hit the Tupperware dish and reaches in to grab it. Just as she is pulling her arm from the freshly dug hole, pain like fire shoots through her hand and up her arm. Instinctively she drops the container, jerking her hand back as blood runs down her forearm, and she hears a familiar rattle, the Tupperware container still in its hole. The note, she has to hold the note, has to feel it in her hands, has to read it one last time. She has to remind herself that it had been real, that all of this hadn't been for nothing. Reaching in for a second time, she is determined to be quicker than a rattlesnake, only she isn't. She wraps her fingers tightly around the container, and leaps back just as a second strike hits her forearm. This time she pulls back with the note safely in her hand. Her heart races, lava coursing through her veins. She backs away from the hole and stands up just in time to see the diamondback rattlesnake scurry back into the thick of the sweet potato patch. Her arm is already swelling, and she feels like she reached her hand straight into a fire.

Maya grabs the bag with her good hand and makes her way towards one of the live oaks. Knowing she has to slow down her heart rate, she starts to breathe slow and easy, concentrating as her chest rises and falls. She reaches in her bag and pulls out her cell phone to check if just maybe, by some miracle, her cell phone has service, but this is Goethe. The only place that she knows of that gets service is down on the south end near the mansion. She knows it is a mile and a half walk back to The Cottages, and then it occurs to her that she doesn't have to go back. She doesn't have anything to go back to, and in that moment she makes the decision to stay. She puts the cell phone down and takes the Nalgene bottle from her bag to drink the rest of the moonshine to help ease the pain. Holding the Tupperware container with one hand, she uses her teeth to open the lid and pull out the note. She hasn't seen it since the day she buried it there five years ago. She holds it close to her heart, tears running down her face. How had everything fallen apart? Remembering the words that she had held in her heart, she reads it over and over until the world is spinning too fast for her to stand.

The hallucinations begin to set in, blurring reality. She wonders if she's dead or alive or somewhere in between. She feels the tilt of the earth's axis throwing her off balance, and she slides down, resting her back against the tree. Looking up, she's surprised to find TK kneeling in front of her, wearing a light colored suit made of linen, a light blue dress shirt and matching tie. He's never looked more handsome. He pulls her to her feet, holding her swollen poisoned hand as he spins her around, catching the small of her back with his other hand, dipping her face into the moonlight. The warmth of his breath caresses her neck. He spins her again, and she feels the bottom of her dress flare out and then wrap itself around her ankles. She looks down at her off-white gown. The flowing dress, simple and sleeveless, is perfect for an island wedding. He smiles and pulls her close as Jill Scott sings "It's Love," with a live band.

"How'd you get Jill Scott to come to the island?"

He smiles, "I've been planning this moment for years. I wanted it to be perfect."

Family and friends are dancing and laughing. Little kids cut in between them, and TK shoos them away, pulling her closer. "I told you I'd come for you."

"It's too late. You waited too long."

"Are you kidding me? The timing's perfect. I'm gonna chase your heart for the rest of our lives. I'll never leave you." He whispers, "I missed you" in her ear and kisses her in front of everyone. She can taste him.

Giant moss covered live oaks and palm trees are wrapped in twinkling white lights and Japanese paper lanterns hang from branches like full moons. The waves from the ocean crash on the shore leaving the beach covered in glowing plankton, more beautiful than she thinks she could dream. It must be real. There's a fire going on the beach where the men are steaming oysters. People gather around tables covered with low country boil, oysters and crabs. The whole island is there.

He rolls up his sleeves, and she takes in the softness

of his skin against hers. Her hand traces the muscles in his back as he leads her around the dance floor.

"Is this real? Can I trust you?"

"Trust everything," he says.

Somewhere deep inside a voice tells her, "It's just another mirage. Don't settle for what's not real. Keep searching for the Promised Land." She awakens, alone and scared in the dark, her arm throbbing. She starts to shake from the coolness of the night and the shock of the venom. A wave of nausea overcomes her, and she leans to the side where she throws up. She starts to cry, sob. Nose running, head spinning, she looks at her arm, which is so swollen that the skin is beginning to split open, and it feels as though she's been struck by lightning, and as much as her arm hurts, her heart aches a hundred times worse.

She leans back against the tree and cries out, "God, save me." Jill Scott fades away and Corrine Bailey Rae takes the stage. She adjusts the mic and begins singing "Closer." Maya closes her eyes as Levi wraps a warm blanket around her.

"I have something to show you," he says, and he tells her to lie down. She can feel the warmth of his arms move across her back as he uses a Sharpie to sketch out his vision.

She hears a knock at the door and gets up. Levi's standing there holding the strangest mixed bouquet of flowers she's ever seen and two plane tickets to Costa Rica. She lies on a surfboard in the middle of the ocean screaming, "No, no, I don't wanna do it! I changed my mind! These waves are too powerful! I'm scared," just as he gives her a big push.

The wave carries her away, and he yells, "You got

this! Stand up! Stand up! You can do it!" and the next thing she knows she's flying across the top of the water all the way to the shore and looks back to see him cheering at the top of his lungs.

She's free.

She sinks beneath the warm water watching the sun break through the surface. She searches for the light and finds it coming through the door of her classroom. Time is running out. She inserts the key and turns. Pushing the door open, she breaks the surface of the water just as she feels her lungs might burst. Drenched, she walks to the front of the room where a dry erase board is covered with a giant pink heart made of Post-It notes. She peels off a square and reads the back, "Independent," and then another and another and another, "Creative. Intelligent. Beautiful." A breeze comes through the window, rustling the Post-It notes as they come to life, magically transforming into butterflies. She stands amazed as they take flight.

Her classroom disappears and she turns around, finding herself in a ballroom. Music is playing. People are dancing and laughing and having a good time. She's wearing her favorite cocktail dress, the black strapless one with the off white embroidered flowers across the top. Sitting alone at a table, she hears Levi's voice, nervous and excited, from behind. She turns to see his hand outstretched. He dances with her, his greatest fear, making a fool of himself in front of everyone just because he knows dancing is her favorite thing, and it makes her smile.

The ballroom disappears, and she is faced with a mirror.

She stares at her reflection, completely exposed, forced to face the truth. Eyes sunken and dark, she takes in the scars where there used to be life, and she begins to cry, her heart hurts. Levi holds her and tells her she's the most beautiful woman he's ever known and that there's so much more to her. He reassures her that God will make her whole again someday. She's sicker than she ever knew a living person could be. He catches her between bouts of vomiting, helping her back to the bed where he lies beside her, dreaming aloud of the future. She closes her eyes to rest. She can hear the waves. He says, "Look! There!" They lie in the dunes watching stars shoot across the sky, and every wish that he makes is for her.

He keeps coming back for her again and again, the way the ocean relentlessly chases the shore. He loves her. He really loves her.

The pain disappears. The pain in her arm, the pain in her soul… gone. She looks at her hand. It's flawless, and then to her shoulder, which now blooms in colors more vibrant than she ever imagined. She realizes that she was always part of creation, a masterpiece. She's whole. A voice calls, "Welcome home, child," and then she sees His face, her true love, just like the dream she had longed to remember and yet couldn't forget. His love washes over her like wave. There are small things, subtle things that remind her of Levi, something in His smile, something about the way He looks at her.

Life begins. New. Perfect. Beautiful. Real. She's in the Promised Land.

CPSIA information can be obtained at www.ICGtesting.com
Printed in the USA
BVOW06s0248191016

465379BV00014BA/168/P